Mist
in the
Blue Bottle

by Ronald J. Bonett

Disclaimer:
This is a work of fiction. All the characters and events
are purely fictional. Business locations and organizations
while real- are used in a way that is purely fictional.

Credits:
Marie Bonett, Bonnie Bell Hilfiger,
Mary Morris for content approval.

Editor:
Rachel Heitzenrater

Introduction

Mist in the Blue Bottle, is a sequel to "Mystery of the Windowed Closet."

The ancient bottle able to reassemble itself after being smashed against the wall by an evil spirit after a séance, has more than just super natural powers, it borders on being unholy. The bottle seemed to take on a life of its own, after sensing the psychic ability of Susan. Through that ability, the bottle charts her on a course where she's able to peer into the strange mist inside the bottle, and thumb through the pages of history.

George, the bottles owner, on his death bed, wills the strange bottle and antique dressing bureau of his grandmother to Susan as a dying gesture. After Susan becomes the benefactor, she and Ray, her boyfriend, move the dresser to her home in Philadelphia.

Polishing her new possession, she discovers an old leather bound folder under the center drawer. Retrieving it, she reads the strange words that were written inside, words that had no meaning. Reading them aloud, they sounded like words that would accompany a ritual of some sort. With the aid of the blue bottle, she was able to take a glimpse into that world then return freely.

When she sees images being projected in the mirror from the bottle, she becomes captivated at her ability to move at will into the scenes.

A chance meeting at a public library with a well dressed elderly man by the name of Justin Stephens sends her ability of entering the dark pages of history to new heights. Without realizing it, she's being lured in. Is she being lured in to take the place of someone but who? Is it her psychic ability that's needed to fulfill a ritual as ancient as the bottle itself? What can the ritual be, and for what purpose? Being drawn in ever deeper, she's being guided away from the relationship with her boyfriend Ray and lifelong friends she knew. How will she escape?

Chapter 1

I opened the front door of my apartment building that windy, drizzly rainy day in November, and looked across the parking lot to where my car was parked. Unfurling my umbrella, I successfully navigated around the puddles, hoping the wind wouldn't turn my umbrella inside out. After getting in, I started the engine and waited a few minutes for it to warm. Rubbing my hands together, I shivered, thinking to myself, "I hate seeing winter coming."

I thought about taking a trip to the farm to close it for the season. I hadn't been there for over a month, since the weekend I had my friends Susan, Delores and Don with me. The series of séances seemed to rid my home of the spirits occupying it. Thinking again, "I wonder if Sue would want to make the trip with me, she did say she wouldn't mind. I'll give her a call this evening. I haven't seen or heard from her since that weekend. I hope she doesn't think I'm not interested."

I had been too busy writing insurance policies and hadn't had much of a chance to dwell on thinking about the farm, or for that matter, any other social functions. Arriving at the office building, I entered the crowded elevator pushing the button for the 4th floor. Just before the door closed, I saw Warren Simmons coming toward the elevator engrossed in reading a policy, and pushed the button to hold the doors open until he was in. He looked up surprised, as though he just realized for some strange reason he arrived at his intended destination.

"Good morning Warren. You must have gotten to work early," I said.

"Yes, I'm looking over this policy. I think this person filed a claim for a fire a few years ago, I just want to check."

"That's good, go get'em tiger," I said jokingly.

It brought a muted laughter from the other elevator occupants. One of them said, "Warren, all you need now is a Bat Man suit, and a companion named Robin."

Everyone chuckled, and Warren turned to look, wondering whether he may have been serious.

"Don't listen to them Warren," I said, "You're one of the constants in a sea of change. You'll take Mr. Johnson's place one day, and be their boss."

"Thanks Ray, I can always count on you to back me up. Don't forget to winterize that farm before winter sets in. I looked at a claim yesterday from last winter. A guy that has a place in the Poconos forgot, and returned in the spring to a ruined house."

"As a matter of fact, Warren, I was just thinking about that this morning. I'll probably head up this Friday after work."

The doors opened and just as though we were suddenly freed from a long captivity, everyone quickly headed in different directions to their respective offices.

Deeply engrossed in my work, I hadn't noticed the time slipped by so quickly. I had worked straight through lunch. I thought, "Should I bother this late in the day? No. I have an idea. Why don't I call Susan and ask if she'd like to go to dinner? I have her phone number where she works somewhere, now where is it?" Rooting through my desk drawer I finally found it. After dialing the number, I received a phone message that she was temporarily away from her desk. I left a message with my phone number and resumed working. Within 15 minutes, the phone rang. "Hello, Ray Bishop, Keystone Insurance. How can I help you?"

"Ray, this is Susan. I was beginning to think I'd never hear from you. Do you have another spirit you want me to exorcise?"

"No Sue, I've been just swamped with work. Since the financial crisis is over, things are beginning to pick up again. I've written probably 20 major policies last week alone. I missed lunch today being so busy, and thought you might like to join me for dinner."

"I'm not doing anything in particular, what time and where shall we meet?" she asked.

"Why don't you pick the spot and tell me. I'm free after 5:00."

"Ok, how about Porter's Restaurant at 15th and Walnut," she suggested, "I'll be there at 5:30."

"I'll see you then," I replied.

After cradling the phone, I looked down at the paper on my desk. I had subconsciously block lettered her name... *SUSAN*.

A pang of hunger suddenly hit my stomach, and looking up at the clock, I realized it was still several hours before dinner. Rooting around in my desk drawer again, I found an unopened pack of peanut butter crackers. Retrieving a soda from the small refrigerator in my office, I indulged.

After writing another policy and looking over the one I had just completed for Mr. Johnson's approval, my work for the day was finished. Looking out the window, the rain had stopped and the clouds were beginning to break, opening up a clearing late afternoon sky.

Taking a last look around the room to see if everything was in order, satisfied, I turned out the light and closed the door. The crowd outside the elevator made me pause and I decided to take the stairs. The walk would be good exercise; it's not often I get the chance. I thought, "Maybe I should just walk to the restaurant? It's only several blocks. It's getting cooler but it isn't raining." With that thought in mind, I took the stairs and exited the building.

Entering the restaurant, Sue was sitting at a bench in the lobby waiting for me.

"Hi there, I hope I haven't kept you too long, I decided to walk."

"No, that's fine Ray. I should do more walking too. It's just that I'm always cold, especially seeing winter come," she pretended to shiver with those words.

"I know the feeling. To be quite truthful, that's one of the reasons I called."

"I knew it. I suspected you have another spirit for me to exorcise."

"No. Not really." I stopped for a moment when the maitre d approached, and ushered us to a table.

After helping her remove her coat, we sat down. The waiter came to the table handing us menus, then took our order for drinks. After opening the menu, Sue quickly closed it humorously remarking, "Too expensive, let's go to the Chatterbox."

Laughing I replied, "That brings up a good point, Chatterbox, Canton, the farm. Just before we were ushered to the table, I was about to ask if you could go to the farm this weekend. I have to close it for the winter."

"Well, to be honest, I have another date," she said examining my face, waiting for my reaction. I must have looked disappointed, and before I could reply she said, "I was only kidding. Sure I'll go. What time do you want to pick me up?"

"How about Saturday at 9:00 a.m.?"

"Won't that be sort of a rush? If we don't get there until mid- afternoon, that won't give you much time to get it done. We'll have to leave the next morning."

"Well, I didn't want to impose too much, I could take off Friday. How about you? Will you be able to get the day off?"

"I won't have a problem with it. All I have to re-schedule is a reading I have Friday evening."

"Just a reading: no exorcism?" I asked.

"Just a reading; Have you seen or heard from Don or Delores lately?" I asked.

"Yes, I have. In fact, Delores called the week after as Frank said, 'Scare the hell out of me weekend.' She wanted to know if you called me, and sounded disappointed when I told her you hadn't. She asked if I wanted her to call you, just to remind you I was waiting."

"And what did you tell her? Were you waiting?" I asked with a sly look.

Looking up with a sheepish smile, she said, "I told her no, but I have to confess Ray, I was lying."

The waiter returned to the table with our drinks and took our food order.

Continuing our conversation, I said, "I imagine what I have to do won't take very long. I'll have to stop at Frank's and ask what I'm supposed to do. It was his parent's house and I'm sure he knows the process. I'll take a few tools with me to do the job, and a few other small items I can move up, that won't be in the way while I'm working on the place come spring."

"Do you want me to bring anything, like cleaning products?" she asked.

"I think Delores bought everything we needed the first time she was there. I don't intend on staying at the house or do much in the way of cleaning. It would be kind of a waste of time. I'm going to start major renovations in the spring, and that's going to create quite a mess."

"Ok, if you insist. I'll just bring the clothes I'm going to need for the weekend."

Over small talk we finished dinner.

As we were getting ready to leave I asked, "Did you drive here?"

"No, I walked too. My office is only two blocks away on Pine Street. Besides, I take public transportation to center city. It's too expensive to park, and the hassle of finding a parking spot just isn't worth the aggravation."

"I know what you mean. If it wasn't for the company parking lot across the street from our building, I'd do the same thing. You won't have to wait for a bus tonight though, I'll drive you home."

After helping her with her coat, we left. Getting outside, the blustery wind was much cooler. The sidewalk and street were almost dry, and she pulled the collar of her coat tight together as we walked briskly to the company parking lot. After getting in the car, she shivered again. In a few minutes, the car began to warm, and I pulled out onto the street.

Arriving at her home she was about to get out of the car when I said, "I'll call you Thursday evening, just to make sure everything's still a- go."

"Ok, you do that."

***

Thursday evening, I called to verify Friday's schedule, and agreed to pick her up at her home in the Northeast section of the city. Actually, it's about three blocks from my former home. Her being divorced, as I was, she probably got the house as part of the settlement just as Jennifer, my ex had. Pulling into the driveway, she opened the garage door with the remote control from inside. I could see the garage was impeccable, as the outside of her home and grounds. The garage wasn't at all like my home with Jennifer. With my garage, it was almost a necessity to have a map to find anything, where hers looked well organized.

Coming from the garage, she waved. Looking at her watch she said, "Good morning Ray; you're punctual. I want you to look at a few things you might want to take. They're tools my ex left. He said he didn't want them."

Getting out of the car, I examined them and put them in the trunk.

"Susan, do you have your clothing bag? I'll put that in the back seat with mine. I don't want to get anything soiled by putting them in the trunk with the tools."

"Yes, I'll get them. They're right inside the door."

"I'll get them for you," I said, "And by the way, you look nice this morning. I like your hair pulled back with that hair band."

"Thanks," she replied before going back inside, "I just want to make sure everything's locked. I'll come out through the garage."

After putting her bags in the back seat, I waited for a few minutes. She exited the garage closing the door with the remote, then got in the car and put the remote in the glove compartment.

"I'm glad the rain stopped, but I could have passed on this cold air that replaced it. It feels good getting into a warm car," she said.

Surveying the outside of the house as I backed out of the driveway, I put the car in drive, slowly looking over the house again as we drove away.

"Sue, how about a coffee to go before we hit the turnpike?"

"That sounds good. There's a place on the Roosevelt Blvd. just before the turnpike entrance."

"I know; I'm familiar with it."

After getting the coffee, I turned into the turnpike approach, and stopped at the toll booth. After saying, "Good morning!" I took the ticket from the toll attendant. Pulling away I said, "Well, Sue, we're on our way. I'm sure glad you were able to take the day off. You were right. Leaving tomorrow morning wouldn't leave much time for getting things done."

"Ray, I had another motive for going today."

Bewildered I asked, "What was that?"

"I'd like to go back to that bar this evening. The one we stopped at with Delores and Don. I thought that was a pretty cool place. Didn't you notice? I'm wearing cowgirl boots."

Looking down at her feet, I said, "I'll be damned. I knew there was something different. I never noticed the boots, but you did seem a little taller. You didn't buy them for this occasion did you?"

"No, I've had them for awhile. After we came back from that weekend, I took them out of the closet and cleaned them. I thought it might be fun to wear if we went back."

"That means you were really anticipating a call from me?"

Avoiding eye contact, she said, "Kind of, but when I didn't hear from you, I put them back in the closet."

"Well, I wouldn't want you to do all that trouble for nothing, It's a deal."

Turning to look at me, she smiled.

Most of our conversation on the drive was about my plans for the house and the séances to exorcise the spirits. Her questions indicated to me she may be interested in a long term relationship, and I was happy with that feeling. A feeling I hadn't had since my divorce.

Driving through the Poconos, the trees had shed all but a few leaves that were stubbornly holding on, defying winters approach. I was sure the rest of the trip would look the same- barren and bleak, waiting for the first snow that makes winter official.

"Sue, I want to stop at Frank's and see if he has a little time to spare tomorrow."

"That's fine. I figured you'd have to do that."

Pulling into his driveway, I could see him at his garage working on a bulldozer.

Frank seemed to be very mechanically inclined, and I know he must save thousands by not having to hire a mechanic. I was almost sure I'd be able to lean on him for a few projects I had in mind during the renovation of the farm. Noticing my car, he looked up putting down the wrench he was using. Taking a rag from his back pocket, he wiped the grease from his hands as he approached.

"Hello Ray. Coming to close the place for the winter?"

"Yes, Frank, that's why I'm here. I'm not sure what to do. Think you can spare some time tomorrow?"

He replied, "I told June last night I should call and let you know we had a few nights where the temperature got below freezing. I know that house doesn't have a lot of insulation. It wouldn't take too much to freeze a water pipe. I didn't think you'd be staying there overnight, what time do you want me to come over?"

"How about 10:00?" I asked.

"That's fine. I'll bring a few tools we'll need. Sue, you look like you're cold. June's in the house, why don't you go in. I'm sure she'd like to see you. I just want to talk to Ray a little while."

"Thanks Frank, I'll do that," she replied.

I realized his request was more than just talking about winterizing the house, and after she walked away, Frank said, "Ray, I didn't want to say anything in front of Sue, but George isn't doing to good."

I quickly asked, "It doesn't have anything to do with the séances. Does it?"

"I don't think so. Ed Jones told me he fell walking through the yard a week after the séances. It laid him up for almost a week. June and another neighbor have been taking care of him, you know, cooking his meals and visiting every day.

I'm sure he'd appreciate a visit from you."

"I was going to do that while I'm here anyway. He's a great guy."

After our conversation we headed for the house. When Frank opened the kitchen door, the aroma of freshly brewed coffee was strong. June was taking a tray of cookies from the oven and looked up addressing Frank, "I guess you must have smelled these cookies were done, clean up by the garage?"

I remarked, "Well June, if he didn't, I sure did. They smell pretty good."

"Have a seat, I'll pour you some coffee and put a few on a plate for you," she replied.

"Thanks, June, I appreciate that. Has Sue been talking about her past experiences?"

"Yes, she has, I think it's fascinating. I went to the library after that weekend and checked out a few books on the subject."

"Did you learn anything from them?" I asked.

"Yes. I learned to stay away from trying to do it. Some of those stories, if they're true, are horrifying."

Sue laughed, "That's because a psychic is only used as a medium. If you're not psychic, what happened to Don could be the result. His inner personality wasn't strong enough to defend itself from the harmful spirit invasion."

I asked, "Then does that mean if a person without psychic ability is in a place where a harmful spirit abides, they can be taken over without being aware of it?"

Sue replied, "They probably wouldn't notice it themselves, but people that know the person, should definitely notice the change in their character."

Frank got up from the table and opened the refrigerator door, he began moving things around and June asked, "What are you looking for?"

He replied as he reached for the milk carton then held it up, "This, you forgot to put out the milk."

June annoyingly said, "I put the milk in a pitcher, it's here on the table."

"I didn't notice," he replied before sitting back down.

June began to tell Susan how much she was able to discover from older people that lived in the community. Some had personal experiences to relate, but the majority was from stories they had heard being passed down from generation to generation. Sue replied, "You can't always believe what a person was told from generations before. There's always a certain amount of drama attached by each generation."

Frank interrupted, "This conversation's giving me goose bumps. Let's change the subject. June, I told Ray about George's failing health. Ray said he wanted to visit with him this weekend, what do you think?"

Sue quickly responded looking at June, "What's wrong with George, is he sick?"

June replied, "No, he fell just after the weekend of the séance and hurt his leg, but I don't think that's what the problem is. Old George is over 90 and some here say he's even older than that, closer to a 100. I don't think he even knows for sure. Me, and one of his neighbors have been lookin' in on him since it happened."

Turning around looking at the grandfather's clock in the dining room, June continued, "I got back about an hour and a half before you came. In fact, I was making these cookies for Frank and George. Since you're going to visit, you can bring them."

Sue asked, "Do you think he needs anything else, we can pick it up on the way?"

"I don't think so. I think he lives off Campbell's Chicken Noodle Soup. That's probably why he's as old as he is. They always say- "Chicken soup is good for what ails ya."

Sue and I laughed. "We know, Sue made him lunch once with a can of it. As I recall, he said he was out of crackers that day. Do you know if he needs any?"

June replied, "I never thought to check. Maybe you can stop at the store on the way and buy some just in case."

Getting up from the table, we thanked June for the coffee and cookies. After putting on our coats, I said, "Frank, I'll see you about 10:00 tomorrow morning."

"Ok, Ray; I'll be here."

Walking to the car, Susan asked, "Do you think George will mind the company?"

"No, I think he'll be fine with it."

"I hope so. I've taken such a liking to the old man."

After buying the crackers, and a few more cans of his favorite soup, we headed for his house.

Pulling into his driveway, to our surprise, he was sitting in his chair on the back porch with only a light sweater on. Getting out of the car, Sue quickly ran to the porch.

"George, you're only wearing a light sweater, that's not enough to keep you warm. Here, let me help you inside."

He replied in a shaky voice a little incoherent, "I didn't know who you were. You look like my old school teacher, boy, was I ever in love with her."

Sue smiled, "Here, let me get you inside. Did you eat today? If you didn't, we brought you your favorite soup, chicken noodle. We brought some crackers too in case you didn't have any."

"I sure like chicken soup, could you put some on for me? I'm not feeling too good today, that's why I came out on the porch."

"Who's that fella with ya?"

Looking at each other, we realized he was much worse than we suspected. He had a dramatic change since we last saw him, and it seemed as though his physical strength as well as his mind seemed to be slipping away.

Sue remarked, "This is Ray, remember? He's the one that moved into Frank's mother and father's house."

George replied, "Frank's mother and father? They've been dead for years. I remember them though. I use to sell them eggs and butter from the back of my old station wagon. My missus used to churn the butter by hand. She sure was some good woman!"

He was remembering things from his distant past, but somehow lost the ability to remember things from a few short weeks ago.

Leading him into the house, we sat him in a kitchen chair. The first thing we noticed, the house was cold. Sue began to open a can of soup and I retrieved the pot and a bowl from the cabinet. He was still examining me and I realized he was beginning to recognize my face, but didn't know the occasion. I helped him with the thought.

"George, I'm the one that came here with Frank when you were sorting apples on the back porch, remember?"

"Oh yeah, now I do, we were in your kitchen when the dishes started falling out of the cabinet. Did you ever fix the shelf?"

I realized at that point, he wasn't aware of the occasion, and let it go at that.

Sue finished preparing his soup and set it in front of him. He didn't seem to have a problem with his hands, they still seemed pretty steady.

Sue said, "Here George, have some of this, it will make you feel better."

To our surprise, his ailments had no affect on his appetite. He dove into the bowl as a kid in a candy dish.

Sue said, "George, I have a surprise for you."

He temporarily stopped eating and looked up at her.

"What's the surprise?"

"June gave me a bag of cookies to give you. I think they're chocolate chip."

He quickly replied, "Well, beggars can't be choosey," then returned to his bowl of soup, scraping the bottom with the spoon until the last drop was scooped up.

"George, can I get you anything else?"

"Just a cup of milk to go with these cookies."

Even though his mind was failing, he still remembered milk is the best companion with chocolate chip cookies. Within 15 minutes after eating, he seemed to be a little more cognizant of who we were. Suddenly, as if I had just entered the room he said, "I know you. You're name's Ray, Frank's neighbor."

"That's right. How are you feeling now?"

"I feel a little better, just cold though."

"Well, George, there's no fire in your stove, I'll light one."

Going into the living room, I looked at the pot belly stove. The metal was cold as ice, and it was obvious he hadn't had a fire going today. I took some newspaper he had stacked near the stove and crumpled it up, putting it in. There was some dry kindling next to the paper and I gently stacked 6 pieces on top of it. Looking around, I didn't see any matches to light it with, and asked, "George, where's the matches?"

"They're in the drawer next to the sofa."

I opened the drawer, and there they were. He remembered, and that was a good sign. I put the lighted match to the paper, and the flames began to spread along the fibers of the kindling. Within a few minutes the warmth began to fill the room. Sue escorted him into the living room and sat him at one end of the sofa.

"Look, Ray, there's the blue bottle on that end table over there," she said.

Looking at it sent a chill up my spine. The feeling was definitely real. It seemed to loom over the room with a sense of foreboding.

I asked, "George, why is the bottle in here? I thought you only kept it on your grandmother's dressing bureau?"

Turning as though he just realized it was present, he said, "I know. When I went to bed last night it was there. It must have followed me."

Sue and I looked at each other, "I remember you telling us it had mystical powers to move on its own," Sue said.

Picking up the bottle, she examined it. "Look, Ray, look at the mist inside the bottle," then handed it to me. I held it to the light coming from the stove, but it was crystal clear. Although the bottle was convoluted by being hand blown as they once were, all I could see through it was a room shaded in blue.

"What mist?" I replied, turning the bottle upside down.

George frightened us when he suddenly shouted, "Don't do that! It don't like being upside down," waving his finger as a parent would disciplining a child. "You can lay it on its side, but not upside down."

Heeding his warning, I quickly put the bottle back on the end table.

Sue said, "George, you frightened us. How do you know that? Will some kind of harm come to the person that does it?"

Looking up at Sue, he replied, "My wife put it in the trunk when she wanted me to get rid of it and I refused. She kept having little mishaps."

"What do you mean mishaps?" I asked.

"Little things, like dropping things when she was trying to make dinner, or tripping over the rug when she shouldn't have. She would lay something down, and when she turned to get it, it moved to somewhere else. That's when she wanted me to throw it in the river. I almost did though. I went to the trunk to get it and noticed it was upside down. After I thought about not throwing it away, I put it back right side up, and my wife didn't have any more mishaps. That's all I know. I sure wish I would have asked my grandmother more about it, and the words she use to say as she brushed out her long hair. You want to hear something funny- her hair never turned gray."

Sue asked as she examined the blue bottle, "George, that's a strange story, how old was she when she died?"

"Well, she didn't really know, but she was probably close to 90 or 100."

Sue asked, "And you say her hair never turned gray, even as she aged?"

"No. She lived here all her life. When my wife and I got married, we moved in with her. She was old then, and didn't have no one else. She was too old to take care of herself, so it worked out. I remember the day she was laid out right here in the living room. Her hair was blond, just as if she was 20 or 30."

Sue asked, "Is that why the dresser is still here?"

"Yes. That was her room where the dresser is now," looking up at Sue, he continued, "You sure looked interested in that blue bottle you're holding at the séance at Ray's. I'll tell you what young lady. If you get me a pencil and paper, I'll write down that I will the dresser, the seat and the blue bottle to you after I die, and sign it. How's that."

Grasping his hand she said, "George, you don't have to do that. How about your relatives, wouldn't one of them want it?"

"I don't have any living relatives. I'm the last one. I want you to have it."

"Thank you George, but you'll live a long time yet."

Looking at her, he smiled realizing they were just kind words.

George reminiscing said, "When I was a youngster, I used to sit on the floor and watch her brush out her hair. She would say words I couldn't understand. I wish I would have asked her more about it. I just didn't think of it at the time. She always said things that made a lot of sense though."

"What do you mean, George?" I asked.

"I remember asking her one day if she was going to die and leave me. She said, 'I'm like yesterday's flower. I have to die to make way for the new.' I didn't know what she meant at the time like most young kids, but as I grew up and saw my friends die, then my wife, I realized the wisdom in those words. I feel comfortable remembering them. Like yesterday's flower, I'm at the end, and I know it."

Directing her to where he kept a pencil and paper, she wrote it exactly as he dictated. Placing it in front of him, he signed where she indicated.

Giving him a hug, she said, "Thank you George. I'll cherish it always, as I will the memory of knowing you."

With that, we saw to whatever he needed, then left. Walking down the stone path, I looked back and couldn't help but feeling sorry for having to leave. I thought, "Maybe, it's not such a good thing to grow so old feeling lonely." I think I probably felt worse for leaving him, than he felt waiting for the hand of death to relieve him of his loneliness.

Driving back to the farm, neither of us spoke, and I could only imagine

Sue felt as solemn as me.

Pulling up in front of the barn, we walked up the hill to the porch. Turning and looking at the valley below, she commented, "It sure looks different from the last time we were here; it's barren and bleak."

"Yes, it seems like autumn's a tease with all the color; it only lasts a short time," I replied.

We entered the house, and I could hear the furnace cranking out a little heat. I had the thermostat turned down to 50 to conserve fuel in my absence.

"Ray, what are you going to do here? Frank said he'd be here tomorrow?" she asked.

"I know. I just wanted to check the place, and bring the tools in from the trunk."

"I'll help," She replied.

"Thanks!"

After putting them in the dining room, we took a tour through the house. Getting to the landing, I opened the door to the closet with the window, half expecting to see something. I was almost disappointed when there were no mysterious breezes across my face. After closing the door I said, "Sue, I guess we successfully exorcised them. Everything else seemed to be the way it was when we left a month ago."

I told her to wait in the kitchen, while I went to the basement to look things over. Checking the fuel in the oil tank, the gage read half full. Here again, no mysterious breezes, and no power surge with light bulbs exploding. I felt good about that, and returned to the kitchen.

I noticed Sue examining the broken cabinet door again from the séance.

I said, "Sue, no mysterious breezes on the second floor, and none in the basement. You did a great job."

For a moment I thought she said something, and asked. "What was that? I didn't hear you."

Looking up from the broken door, she replied, "I didn't say anything. What did you think I said?"

"I'm not sure. It sounded like you said, 'Where are you Davey,' like you were talking to a kid."

"That's funny, for some strange reason the name David crossed my mind. I don't know why, I don't think I even know any Davids."

"If you were thinking about it, maybe you subconsciously said it."

"Maybe, that's the only thing I can think of. Did everything in the basement look ok?"

"Yes, just as it did when you and Delores went down, a mess."

"Well, what are we going to do the rest of the day?"

"I was thinking about driving to Towanda to get familiar with the area. We'll have to check into a motel for tonight too. How does that sound?"

"That sounds good as long as there's a lunch on our travels."

Looking at my watch, I said, "I didn't realize the time. I think the Chatterbox closes at 2:00, but I can manage a late lunch somewhere."

Taking a last look around, I locked the door.

Chapter 2

Towanda, is a small city of about 28,000 people. Actually, the town is divided in two by the Susquehanna River. The far side from the town is a small community called Wysox. With the exception of a few homes, it's largely a commercial strip they refer to as The "Golden Mile." Three auto sales establishments and a shopping mall are a large part of it, with a few independent stores, two motels, and three fast food restaurants.

Seeing a small diner at the intersection dissecting The Golden Mile, we noticed the parking lot was full. A relic from the late 40's or early 50's, it was complete with a rounded roof and windows the length of one side.

"Look Ray, that seems to be where a lot of people are eating, let's try it."

"I guess with all the cars and pickup trucks, they're probably locals, it should be a sure bet," I replied.

After pulling into the parking lot, we entered. The inside was exactly as one would expect from that era, a long counter with swivel stools, and booths along the window. The coffee urns were prominent along the back wall behind the counter, and two waitresses were busy running back and forth from customer to kitchen, with trays of food. We spotted an empty booth along the window side, and a waitress seeing us looking in that direction, smiled, then announced. "Better take it while it's empty, seats are in short supply today."

Taking her advice just as someone else entered the restaurant, we sat down.

"Look, Sue, a table side jukebox. I haven't seen one of these in ages. Let me scan it to see what kind of music they're offering."

"I'll bet its country music like we heard at that bar," she replied.

"I don't think I'll take that bet. I know I'll lose."

Opening the menu, the prices didn't vary far from the prices at the Chatterbox.

"Sue what do you think you're going to order? They're giving us a choice of lunch or dinner."

"Since it's too late for lunch, I think I'll order an early dinner. That looks like what everyone else is having. The chalk board behind the counter is advertising the special- meat loaf with mashed. I think I'll try it."

That was another positive I noticed about her, my ex would have never wanted to eat in a place like this, and would have definitely never ordered the special. I was beginning to realize she was the sort of person I could be in tune with. Someone that wasn't a- *'me first'* person.

The meal was very good, and I put the establishment on my list for a future visit. Leaving, we went to the Comfort Inn to secure rooms for the night. Upon our entry the desk clerk asked, *"One room or two?"*

I looked at Sue then smiled, "Your choice!"

Disappointedly she replied, "Two rooms if you please, but if they're adjoining, I won't mind."

With a smile I said, "That sounds positive."

"No, just a matter of convenience if we have to discuss something."

My expectations were quickly dashed, but I was impressed she didn't want an intimate relationship so soon after we met.

It was already 4:00, and there didn't seem to be anything left to do that day. After a cup of coffee at a local shop she said, "I think I'd like to go back to the motel."

"I hope it's not the company?"

"No, for some strange reason today's been really tiring for me, I feel completely drained. I think I just want to lie back for awhile."

"Do you think dealing with George could have made you emotionally drained? I know it affected me."

"I don't think so. Oh sure, I felt bad about his position, and I'm sure you do too, but it seems like after we left your house, is when it all of a sudden hit me. I don't know why."

"Maybe you should lie down and take a nap. That dinner was kind of a heavy meal."

"Maybe I'll do that, you won't mind will you?"

"No, I think I'll do the same. With me, the perfect sleep aid is watching TV."

After a few more words we decided to go to our *separate* rooms.

As I mentioned to Sue, the greatest sedative for sleep, is watching television. Leaning on my pillows propped against the headboard, I soon drifted off to sleep. I was awoken by the lamenting sound of a woman crying. Her words were undistinguishable and in the darkened room, I thought at first it may have been a television program. Sitting up, I realized it couldn't be. At some point during the evening, while I was still half asleep, I must have turned the television off. Rising up further to listen, I followed the direction of the sound. It was coming from Susan's room. I put my ear to the adjoining door and realized, that's where it was coming from. I gently knocked, but there was no reply. I knocked again, this time harder, calling her name. It was enough to wake her, and I could hear the latch on her side of the door open. She was drenched with sweat to the point her hair looked as though she just came from the hotel pool. She was pale and unsteady on her feet, so I held her arm leading her to a chair. I noticed her room was really warm, and looked at the thermostat to turn it down. To my surprise, it was only set on 70 degrees, but the warmth in the room far exceeded that reading.

"Are you ok?"

"Yes, Ray, what happened?"

"You must have had a bad dream. You sounded like you were talking in your sleep and crying."

"That's unusual, I rarely dream. Do you know what I was saying?"

"It sounded like you were saying David again, but I can't be sure. Can I get you anything?"

"A glass of water please. I still feel shaky."

After I brought back the water, I asked, "Sue, do you think it may have something to do with being at George's, or the farm today?"

"I don't know. I don't think so. It seems like I dreamt about the farm, but it's all fuzzy in my mind."

"Maybe it's not a good idea for you to go with me in the morning when I meet Frank."

Her look of trying to understand what she had dreamt was replaced by a look of contempt. I didn't do anything but express my concern for her, so why the look? I decided not to pursue it any further.

"Sue, we'll talk about it in the morning."

"Ok. Thanks for the help."

Retiring to my room, I laid awake thinking of what transpired. Could the farm house be affecting her?

Whatever it was seemed to infect her normally pleasant attitude.

***

In the morning, I was awoken by Sue shaking my shoulder. I opened my eyes to her staring down at my face.

"How did you get in here?" I asked.

"You must have left your side of the door unlatched. I knocked first, but I guess you were so sound asleep, you didn't hear me. You looked so peaceful; I didn't want to wake you."

Leaning up on my elbow, I took my watch from the end table. "It's almost 8:00. I better get showered and dressed. I'll meet you in the dining room in about 20 minutes."

Smiling, she replied, "Ok, I'll keep the coffee warm."

That was the Susan I knew before the dream last night, and I hoped there wouldn't be a repeat. After showering and dressing, I joined her. She was sitting at one of the tables engaged in a conversation with an older couple, and as I approached she introduced me.

"Ray, this is Mister and Missus Thompson. They live in Philadelphia now, but they're originally from Canton. They moved to the city after Mister Thompson retired."

I remarked, "That's a reversal of roles. I live in Philadelphia and want to retire here. I've only recently acquired the place, but I met a few people you may know. Do you happen to know George Burkley, or Frank and June? Now let me think- what's their last name?" failing to remember I continued, "Anyhow, they're my neighbors. I bought Frank's mother and father's old place. It's on Sunset Road. Are you familiar with it?"

Looking at his wife, Mister Thompson replied. "We sure are. We went to school with Frank and June; their last name is Wilson."

"Then you must know Ed Johnson? I met him one day too. He told me him and Frank were in the same grade."

"Yes, we know him too."

Sue poured out two cups of coffee and rejoined our conversation.

Mister Thompson asked, "Since you bought the house, have you had any disturbances?"

"Why do you ask that?" I replied. Looking at Sue, I wondered how much he knew about the disturbances.

"Just asking," he said. "I know Frank's younger sister had a heck of a time there for awhile. I know it was that bad, they had to send her to Frank's Aunt Ethel in Canton every year."

Sue remarked, "Well, it started out to be a problem, but I think we solved it."

Missus Thompson replied, "That house always felt a little too spooky for me. Whenever I was going out with June and had to wait until she was ready, I always felt like someone was watching me."

Mister Thompson added, "Don't mind my wife. She just loves mysteries and horror movies. Come on dear. Let's let these young people drink their coffee in peace."

After making their departure, Susan and I got a few breakfast items and returned to the table. I made it a point not to discuss her not returning to the farm, and after several cups of coffee, we were ready to leave.

Shortly after pulling up in front of the barn, Frank came up the road. "Good morning, Frank, I know I'm 15 minutes late. I hope you didn't give up on me?"

"No, I told June you'd be here any minute, and you were. Let's get to it."

"Frank, the reason I'm late. We ran into a couple that said they knew you and June. Their last name is Thompson."

"Oh, yeah, we go back a long way. I knew they came back for a funeral of a distant cousin on his wife's side, but I didn't get a chance to see them."

I asked Sue, "Why don't you walk down to see June. I'm sure she'd like a visit?"

Frank added, "I know she would. She'll probably pester ya about any séances you had since that night."

After unlocking the door, we went in. I remarked jokingly, "Ok Frank, start instructing."

Raising and lowering his cap, he replied, "Well, there really ain't much to it. We have to start in the basement."

The light bulb was out again and I wondered whether it was a spirit that did it, but Frank, unlike me, thought enough to bring a flashlight.

Reaching over his head, he grasped a valve on a water pipe. "Here's how you turn off the water to the upstairs," turning it to capacity. After opening another valve, he instructed me to open all the faucets in the kitchen and bathroom. I did as he asked and returned to the basement. He opened another valve and the water still held in the pipes, ran out on the dirt floor, causing us to step back. I asked a few questions about the electrical box, and hot water tank, then he instructed me on what to do."

"Is that all there is to it?"

"Not quite. I brought some anti-freeze with me. You have to pour a little in each drain and in the toilet and the water chamber. That will keep it from freezing."

Going back to the kitchen, Sue was sitting in a chair staring at the broken cabinet door again on the kitchen table.

"Sue, I thought you went down to visit June?" I asked.

"No, I changed my mind. Are you finished?"

"I don't know," turning to look at Frank I asked, "Frank, are we finished?"

He was staring at Sue as if he wanted to say something, but his words wouldn't come out. I repeated myself, "Frank, are we finished?"

It brought him out of the deep thought replying, "I'm sorry Ray, yes, we're finished."

"Sue, I think we better go now."

She too, seemed to be at a loss for words, until I repeated myself. All of a sudden she looked up and said, "Yes, David, I'm ready."

"David? Who's David?" I asked.

"Did I say David again Ray? I'm sorry. I don't know why I keep saying that."

Frank looked a little bewildered and broke the conversation. You can both stop down the house after you lock up. I'll tell June to put on the coffee."

Sue replied for us, "No thanks. Frank, I think I want to stay here for awhile. I'd like to visit George again. It's probably the last opportunity before we go back to the city."

"Well, that's up to you. The offer's there."

I was concerned about Susan turning down the offer without my input, but let it go. I walked Frank to the front door and thanked him once again.

He quietly asked, "Is she alright?"

Looking back at Sue over my shoulder, I replied, "She just had a bad night. She'll be fine."

I returned to the kitchen to speak to Susan about her change in attitude, when she suddenly stood up and came toward me. She had a blank look on her face, a face that seemed to be devoid of my presence. I stood aside as she walked by as if I wasn't there. Getting to the bottom of the stairs leading to the 2nd floor she paused. Looking up at the landing she said, "I'm coming David. I'm coming." Then slowly went up. I kept asking who David was, but she didn't turn or seem to hear me. Reaching the landing, she paused again-then turned to the right into the windowed closet. Entering the room, she stood staring at an empty corner, as if there was something there. It was the same corner where I saw the mirage of the bolts of cloth, with the toddler's leg protruding from behind them. I suddenly realized why she was fixated on the corner. In the séances we had to rid the house of spirits, everyone was exorcized, but the toddler and Adda, but aside from a little dust, the room was empty.

Whatever was plaguing her, made her seem like a zombie, controlled at the slightest touch or command. I took her by the arm and led her back down the stairs and out the front door. Once she was on the porch, she seemed to come out of her semi conscious state.

"Ray, are we leaving now?"

I asked, "Do you remember going upstairs to the windowed closet?"

"When did I do that?"

"About 5 minutes ago. Don't you remember?"

"All I remember is listening to you talking to Frank. Did he leave?"

"What's the last thing you remember?" I curiously asked, trying to understand at what point she was influenced by whatever it was directing her.

"I remember Frank telling me to go down to visit June. I was walking down the hill looking forward to it, but for some strange reason, I turned around and came back. That's when I heard you speaking with Frank. It seemed like everything went blurry after that, and I was in a mist. It's hard for me to explain, but that's all I remember until now. I do remember you saying we wanted to visit George. Is that where we're going?"

Locking the front door I replied, "Yes, I think we better get away from this house for awhile."

On the way to George's, I wondered if he could remember if the toddler's name was David. If it is, somehow he'll have to be put to rest as the others were. If Sue said Adda was still present, maybe that's what's keeping her here. The local newspaper was closed for the weekend, but it's over a hundred years in existence, and would probably have the story of the fire in its archives. I decided not to tell Susan I wanted to come back during the week.

"Ray, penny for your thoughts," she asked.

"Oh, I'm sorry Sue, I was thinking about the basement project." I lied, but felt it was necessary. I continued, "I was just giving some serious thought of tearing the house down and starting fresh- What do you think?"

Slowly turning she gave me the same look of contempt she had yesterday, and I expected the same hostile response. Instead, she replied in a more pleasant tone.

"I think that's foolish, we could work on it together."

"Well, it's something I'll have to think about."

A light rain began to fall as we pulled into George's driveway, and I noticed once again there was no smoke coming from the chimney. Exiting the car we hurried to the back porch. Sue knocked on the door but there was no answer. Trying the handle the door was unlocked and we stepped inside. The house was cold and damp, and we found George huddled under several blankets on the living room sofa. His hand felt cold, and I thought at first he passed away, but when I shook his shoulder, his eyes suddenly opened.

"George, you don't have a fire going, I'll light one for you. Have you eaten today?"

"I'm not sure. No, I don't think so."

"Well, Susan's in the kitchen, she's making you something."

He sat up, and as I began to get the stove started. I asked, "George, have you ever given it a thought to have someone stay here with you?"

"Well, here lately I have. I just can't seem to get anything done."

"You said you didn't have any relatives. Why don't you consider selling the farm and moving into that senior center in Canton? It seems like a pretty good place to live, and someone can keep an eye on you."

"Well, I gave it some thought a while back, but I don't like to live crowded, and I don't know any of those people."

"It was just a suggestion, but you should have someone stay with you on a full time basis. You know, make your meals and keep the stove going for you."

He seemed to be pondering my words replying, "I'll think about it."

Sue entered the living room and said, "George, I have something prepared for you to eat." Taking him by the arm, she said, "Here, I'll help you to the kitchen table."

Her concern for him was one of the things I liked- totally unselfish. The swing in her attitude regarding the possibility of keeping her away from the house was beginning to make me worry. Was her psychic ability losing ground to whatever forces were pulling her in a different direction?

Sitting at the kitchen table, I asked, "George, you mentioned there was a fire in my house around 1910, and a young boy died in that fire. Do you happen to remember his name?"

Looking up from his bowl, he said, "Let me think now, I think it was David, but I'm not sure. It's been a long time ago."

Susan remarked, "I have an idea. George do you think the blue bottle will give us the answer?"

"It might. Why don't you go in the bedroom and get it. It's on my grandmother's dresser."

Happy at the thought, she hurried to retrieve it. Coming back to the kitchen, she was staring at the bottle, seemingly mesmerized by it. She asked, "George, do you mind if I take it back to Ray's? We might be able to get June and Frank to join us for a séance tonight."

"Do you want me to come along in case it doesn't work for you? I remember someone borrowed it once and it didn't work for them. I don't remember who it was. Maybe I'll have to be there."

"You're welcome to it, but I don't think you're up to going. Maybe you should stay home," she replied.

He agreed, but offered to go again if it didn't work.

"Ray, I'll have to go to town and get a few candles, then we have to ask June and Frank if they'll do it."

"Whenever you're ready to leave, I am."

After George was finished eating, we were about to leave, when June pulled into the driveway.

"Hi Sue, Ray, you beat me too it. I was coming to see if he needed anything."

"June, when we got here he was huddled under a few blankets asleep on the sofa. The house was cold. That's the second time we came and there wasn't any fire going," repeating myself, "The house was really cold. I'm afraid when winter sets in, if he's still here by himself, there's a possibility he might freeze to death. Someone should see if they can get somebody to stay here on a full time basis, or have George stay with someone."

Looking sympathetically at him she replied, "I tried to talk him into it once, but he said no. I'll ask again. If Frank don't mind- and I'm sure he wouldn't, George could stay with us."

"That's a nice offer," I replied, "By the way, we want to try a séance tonight, are you and Frank up to it?"

Looking surprised, she asked, "Why are you having another séance? Did a spirit come back to the house?"

"No, I think the reason for Adda still being there, is the kid that died in the fire. It's beginning to affect Sue."

"What time do you want us to be there?" June quickly asked.

"How about 7:00?" Sue replied.

"Ok, we'll be there."

After settling the arrangement, we left for town. On the drive, I noticed Sue seemed to be transfixed, staring at the bottle again.

"You're staring at that bottle as if you're hypnotized. Are you?" I asked.

"No, it's just this strange mist I see."

"Mist? Let me see it."

Looking at the bottle, I temporarily lost concentration of my driving, and ran off the side of the rain slick road. Quickly pulling back I said, "That was close. I better concentrate on my driving until we get to town, it's beginning to sleet."

Arriving at the hardware store, we purchased six candles then left for the farm. Before exiting the car, I asked. "Do you have a pencil and paper for the word *YES* and *NO*? If you don't, I have one in the glove compartment."

Searching her purse she replied, "I think I have one. Yes, here it is."

Going into the kitchen, we prepared for the séance. Sue placed the candles in the same locations as the séance's before, then printed *YES* and *NO* on two pieces of paper, placing them at opposite ends of the table. After she put the blue bottle in the center of the table, the bottle seemed to move by itself. After studying it for a few moments, I dismissed it as my imagination. I thought, "If it did move, maybe it's some sort of satisfaction it has a purpose once again." If that's the case, it would be a good indication it may work for Sue, and I couldn't wait for us to find out.

"Sue, we haven't eaten since this morning. It's 2:00 already. Maybe we should drive back to Wysox and eat dinner?"

"That's funny, I don't even feel hungry, but I guess you're right," she replied.

I wondered whether she was in jeopardy of harming herself with everything that's happening. This was supposed to be a relaxing weekend to close the house for the winter, nothing more. Seeing how it was affecting her, I wished I hadn't asked her to come. On the drive to town, it was as though she read my thoughts.

"Don't feel bad that you invited me, I'm enjoying it," she said.

Suddenly, I felt naked, and a horrible thought crossed my mind. If we have a relationship, would I be uncomfortable knowing she could do that?

We stopped at the Fireside Restaurant in Wysox to dine, and after a scrumptious dinner, we returned to the hotel to change clothes.

The drive back to the farm was a little hampered by the sleet falling, and I wondered whether the roads would be icy on our return after the séance. Putting that thought aside, we pulled up in front of the barn. The sleet rapidly was turning into flakes, but the snow was only building up on the lawn and not on the roadway, which eased my mind considerably. Within a few minutes, Frank came up the road and parked behind my vehicle.

"Well Frank, are you ready?"

He replied, "I'm as ready as I'll ever be. June here was watching the clock hoping the time would go a little faster, she's really into this. Sue, I think you created a monster."

After lighting the candles, I placed the small pieces of paper with YES and NO at each end of the table, and turned out the lights. Sue, was at one end of the table, and I was at the other, with Frank and June on opposite sides.

"June, would you ask the questions," Sue asked.

"What kind of questions? I don't know what this is about?"

"We're trying to find out the toddler's name that died in the fire in 1910. We think his name was David, and we want to know why his spirit is still restless. That's why I think Adda is still with us."

"I didn't know you still had a problem. When did this start?" June asked.

I interrupted, "It began yesterday but it became even stronger today."

"Ok, now that I know what it's about. Do you want me to ask just that question, his name?"

"It depends on how he responds. Ask if there's another reason he isn't at rest."

With those words, flickers of light from the candles made our shadows on the wall appear to be moving. If David was his name, and that was his response to hearing his name, we were ready to begin. Sue lowered her head going into a trance, and in a few minutes her hair fluffed up. Like the other séances, we knew Adda through Sue, was ready to answer questions.

"Adda are you with us tonight?" June asked.

The bottle slowly turned to the word *Yes.*

"Adda, is the spirit of the toddler that's still here named David?"

The bottle gently turned again pointing to the word *Yes.*

"Why is he still restless, did something happen that makes him afraid?"

Again, the bottle turned in a complete circle and stopped, pointing to the word *Yes.*

I asked, "What is David afraid of?"

Adda answered "He was playing with matches in the sewing room, that's what started the fire. He was afraid he was going to be spanked, so he hid behind the bolts of cloth. He heard his mother calling, but he was afraid to answer.

I'm trying to save him, but I'm not able. I pick him up and try to wake him, but he's dead. I don't know what to do."

Just then, a shadow appeared on the wall. It wasn't ours. Who was it? A closer look revealed it was the shadow of a woman holding a child in her arms, and we assumed it was Adda. The child's arms and legs looked as though they were dangling, a lifeless body she couldn't save. Was that all there is to this haunting?

June asked, "Is there anything we can do to help?"

The room fell quiet, and we thought the spirits had left. Suddenly Frank began to cry sounding like a toddler. "Mommy, help me. Daddy locked me in the room."

June asked looking at the bottle, "Adda, why was he locked in the room, was he being punished?"

The bottle immediately turned to the word *No.* June continued feverishly. "Then why was he locked in there?"

Slowly Adda spoke in a lamenting voice, "It's not his real father. His mother was re-married and her husband hates children. When David's mother isn't around, he punishes him for no reason," lamenting again, "If I could only take him away."

"Why can't you?" June asked.

"He's held here, looking for something that belonged to his father."

"What is it, can you tell us?"

"It's something I've never seen. He keeps pointing at the floor in the front bedroom, but there's nothing there."

I thought about the money that was hid under the floor board, and the few buttons I found. Could it be that something's under there I missed? I put the question to the blue bottle.

"Did I miss something that was under the floor board?"

The bottle slowly turned to the word *Yes*.

Frank came out of his trance first, and Sue followed shortly.

She asked, "Did you find out anything?"

I replied, "The toddler's name is David, and he has something hidden from his step father under the floor board in the front bedroom. I remember searching under a loose board in that room the first weekend I was here, and found a few buttons. I'll bet whatever it is, it's under that floor board."

Frank replied, "I have a flashlight in the truck, I'll get it and we can take a look."

After coming back, we went upstairs to where I found the buttons. Lifting up the loose floor board, I took the flashlight and peered under. As the light was penetrating the darkened space- something shinny caught my eye. I reached in as far as I could and grasped it. Taking it out, I opened my palm and looked. It was a gold pocket watch. Opening it, there was a picture of a man we assumed was David's real father. The watch was inscribed with the words. 'This I bequeath to David my son. When you look at it remember me.' We were sure a toddler that young wouldn't have been able to read, but no doubt his mother must have told him what the endearing words meant.

Coming back to the kitchen, June anxiously asked, "Did you find anything?"

"Only this," opening my hand, I placed it on the table.

Sue opened it and read the words to June. Frank asked, "Should we set the séance again and see if it helped?"

"That's the only way we'll be able to tell," Sue replied.

Lighting the candles again, we returned to our places. Within a few minutes after Susan lowered her head, she looked up and began to laugh. The laughter was Adda. The shadow we saw on the wall before with her holding a lifeless body had changed. The toddler was now standing next to her, holding her hand looking up at her face and laughing. The shadows walked to the entrance of the kitchen then disappeared. It was over. Everyone was happy with the outcome, especially me. There was no need to critique the séance; it was very plain what had happened. I suspected June wanted to talk about it more, but the only person that commented was Frank.

"I can't believe there was so much spirit activity in the house I grew up in," humorously adding, "I'm glad they never had to be fed. There was hardly enough food to go around as it was."

June added, "Not to mention waiting in that line to use the bathroom." We laughed as we left the kitchen.

"How about coming down for coffee?" June asked.

I was about to say yes, when Sue replied, "We'd like to, but Ray promised to take me to a bar we stopped at the last time we were here. They had great music, and I'm in the mood for some entertainment."

"What bar was that?" June asked.

"If I remember correctly, it was a place called Kelly's."

I looked at Sue with an approving smile. With her changed attitude, I realized what had been affecting her in the house, was gone. Helping her on with her coat, we walked out on the porch. The sleet had stopped and the night sky was crystal clear, revealing a million stars. After locking the door, I said, "Frank, thanks again for showing me how to winterize the place, and helping us with the séance. We'll be heading back to the city in the morning. You have my phone number. If you'd keep an eye on the place during the winter, I'd appreciate it.

At some point, I may just take a ride up just to look for myself, but that will depend on the weather."

June said, "We have your phone number. If anything happens, we'll give you a holler."

Waving goodbye, we got in the car and headed for Kelly's Tavern.

Chapter 3

Pulling into the parking lot of the bar, it was full, and I was about to pull out and park alongside the road with the other vehicles, when I saw a person leaving, and was fortunate enough to be able to get their parking space.

Bow hunting season was over, but rifle season for black bear and deer was only a few days away. The extra vehicles were probably from people that lived elsewhere, and had hunting camps nearby preparing for the season opening.

After entering the bar, it was just as we expected- crowded.

The music from the band was loud, and we stood in the doorway for a few minutes scanning the room for an empty table.

"I don't think we're going to get a table. I'm sorry you went to all the trouble wearing your cowgirl boots, I don't think you'll get a chance to use them." I said.

Just then, someone tapped me on the shoulder. Quickly turning, I realized it was Ruthie, the waitress from the *Chatterbox*.

Raising my voice to be heard over the music and conversations, I said, "Hello Ruthie, this place is really crowded tonight."

"Yeah, it gets that way all the time when hunting season opens. Believe it or not, most of them are flatlanders, just like you."

"What's a flatlander?" Sue asked.

I replied, "That's a reference to someone that's from down country-someone that doesn't live here. I won't have to wear that title in 30 years, I'll be a resident."

Ruthie scanned the room then said, "Let me deliver this tray of food. I see a couple sitting at a table in the back of the room. They're locals, and don't stay very long after the music starts. I'll see if they're ready to leave so you can have their table."

"Thanks Ruthie, we'll wait right here."

Watching her negotiate the crowd with the full tray of food, she resembled a ballerina, maneuvering in and around people with grace to her final destination. We watched as she went to the table with the locals, and saw her speaking with them. Looking in our direction, she waved and we quickly headed toward her.

"Missus and Mr. Wagner, this is Ray," Ruthie said, pausing for a moment. She didn't remember my last name, so I helped, "Bishop's the last name," before I could finish, Ruthie continued, "He bought the old Leona and Wilber Farm. He's from Philadelphia."

I added, "This is Susan, she's a friend of mine."

They were an older couple, I guessed in their early sixties. After we acknowledged each other, they rose from their seats and we quickly took their place. I thanked them and Ruthie for being so considerate, then placed our order.

I noticed Sue tapping her feet in time with the music and asked with a faked southern drawl, "Well Ma'am, how's about a dance?"

In the same southern drawl she replied, "Well Sir, You take my breath away, you surely do. With your offer, I certainly would like to," we both laughed.

Leaving our coats over the backs of our chairs, we headed for the dance floor.

After realizing we couldn't get within 10 feet of it, we stopped, joining the other couples that couldn't get on the floor either, swaying in time with the music. Susan outperformed me once again, but my lack of ability, gave way to the enjoyment of watching her. Getting back to the table after the music stopped, I said, "You looked great. I think other couples were jealous of your ability."

"Well, it's just my cowgirl boots I'm wearing. That's the secret. They put me in the mood. Did you enjoy yourself?"

"Yes!"

We danced several more times within the next few hours, until she said,

"I think I had enough dancing for tonight, I'd like to leave."

"I'm ready too. The noise is beginning to get to me. Here, let me help you with your coat."

After getting in the cold car, she looked down at her boots then stamped her feet, rubbing her hands together, "Boy it's getting cold." Turning to look at me, I took her hands in mine, blowing warm breath on them saying, "The car will be warm in a few minutes."

Our eyes met, and I pulled her close, placing my lips to hers. She responded in kind, and after the kiss, she moved closer holding onto my arm. As I pulled out on the dark road, the car began to warm.

Arriving at the motel, we went inside. A different desk clerk acknowledged our entry saying, "Good evening, can I help you?"

"No, we're already registered," I replied, "Can I get a wakeup call?"

"Certainly, what's your room number?"

"Mine's 212 and hers is___."

I paused momentarily hoping she would say, Mine's the same,' but no offer was made. Before I could finish, she added, "You can call me at room 213."

A broad smile crossed my face and I knew Sue recognized it. Looking at her I asked, "Are you sure?"

"Yes, I'm sure," she replied.

I was disappointed for the second time but didn't protest. We headed to our separate rooms and before entering hers, we kissed again. Looking into my eyes, she said, "Be patient Ray."

"Good night Sue. I'll see you in the morning."

I laid awake for awhile thinking about a possible relationship. She seemed to have all the qualities I wanted, and I think the feeling is mutual. I thought, "Time will tell."

The phone rang at 8:00, and I answered. "Yes, I'm awake, thank you. Did you call 213?"

The operator replied, "No, I haven't."

"That's alright, don't bother, I'll knock at her door."

Gently tapping, I heard her voice from the other side, "I'm awake," and unlatched the door from her side. Opening it, she still looked tired, but I noticed even without makeup, she had a natural beauty.

"I look terrible," she said.

"No, you don't. You have a natural beauty."

Still half asleep, she leaned against the door jamb with her head on her arm replying, "I feel like I could just go back to bed and sleep for a few more hours."

"Well, we don't have to check out until 11 a.m. Why don't you?"

Standing up straight, she shook her head replying, "No, that's alright, I'll be fine. Just let me take a quick shower. I'll meet you in the cafeteria in about 20 minutes."

"Ok, that's a deal."

After getting dressed, I headed for breakfast, and was happy she didn't want to sleep in. I was anxious to get back to the city to go over some insurance policies I brought home. In about 20 minutes, she entered the room.

Looking around, she said, "That coffee smells good."

"Sit down Sue. I'll get you a cup."

After breakfast, we returned to our rooms to get our bags. After taking a last minute survey of the room to make sure we didn't leave anything, I turned out the lights and closed the door. After checking out, I loaded the bags in the trunk then headed for Philadelphia.

"We got everything done I wanted to do. Thanks for your help with exorcizing Adda and David," I said.

"That's alright, I enjoyed the weekend. I hope you'll invite me again after turning you down last night," she said with a smile.

"That's no problem."

"I want you to understand something Ray. I haven't been with a man since my husband and I were divorced. That's more than 8 months ago, and probably 6 or 8 months before that. I'm kind of nervous."

"Don't worry. When it happens, I'm sure you'll be fine."

Changing the subject I said, "You no doubt will tell Delores about the weekend."

"Yes, and I know she's going to be pissed that she wasn't there."

I laughed, as I headed for the turnpike entrance. Several hours later, the city came into view.

Pulling into her driveway, she used the remote to open the garage door. Before getting out, she leaned over caressed my face, then kissed me.

"Thanks for being understanding," she said.

"No problem. Would it be alright if I call you this week?"

"Yes, please do."

That evening around 7:30 as I was looking over the insurance policies, the phone rang. To my surprise it was Susan.

"Ray, I just got off the phone with Delores. She asked if we could come over one night this week for dinner. She's anxious to know what happened. I told her I'd have to check with you first. I'm free this week until Thursday-How about you?"

Looking at my note calendar on my desk, I Jokingly asked, "Ok, who's my competition Thursday evening?" she began to reply when I said, "I'm only kidding. But before I can make a firm commitment, I have to check my schedule at work tomorrow. If I don't have anything scheduled, how about Wednesday?"

"Wednesday's good for me," she replied, "I'll call her back and make it tentative."

"That's alright, I'll call her after I finish talking to you. I want to ask Don a question. Oh, by the way, thanks again for accompanying me this weekend."

"No problem, I enjoyed it."

After hanging up, I called Don. Delores answered the phone and began to speak before she realized it was me, "Sue, what day are you and Ray coming over?"

I replied, "This isn't Sue, but I think it might be Wednesday, I'll call tomorrow evening to confirm things. What's for dinner? Spaghetti I hope!"

"Spaghetti it is. Wait, I'll get Don. He's in the bathroom." I could hear her call out, "Don, Ray's on the phone!"

I heard him reply, "I'll be out in a minute."

While I was waiting for him I asked, "I'll bet you're chomping at the bit wanting to know what happened."

"Yes, I am. Sue told me about George, that's really sad. Here's Don, I'll see you Wednesday; tentatively."

"What can I do for you Ray?" Don asked.

I asked about a potential problem I might have with a policy I wrote, but after a few minutes of conversation, in my mind, it was resolved.

"Thanks Don. I'll probably see you Wednesday."

He asked, "Now that we can speak freely without the girls listening, how did everything work out with Susan?"

"Great, we'll probably start dating. She's really a kind giving person. The way she hovered over George was nothing short of remarkable- totally unselfish."

"Yeah, she is one remarkable girl. Her ex was a real a-hole. I don't know what she ever saw in him. They say beauty is in the eye of the beholder, but the day she met him, she must have been blindfolded."

I laughed, "Well for my sake, I'm glad she took it off. I'll see you Wednesday."

I put down the phone reflecting on my last statement, 'That's right- I am happy as hell she took it off.' After a few more hours of looking over policies, I decided to call it a night.

***

As I stepped out of the elevator at the 4th floor, I encountered my boss Mr. Johnson.

"Good morning Ray. How was your weekend?"

"It was pretty productive Mr. Johnson."

Holding a policy in my hand, I said, "I was looking over this policy last night. I think it's ok. I'd just like to have you look it over in case I missed anything."

Looking at the policy, then at me over his wire rimmed glasses, he replied, "That's what I like about you. You take your work home if it's necessary. I hope you don't mind, but I'm recommending you to take over my position to corporate headquarters when I retire in the spring. How would you like that?"

"That's great Mr. Johnson, but I'm sure the company is going to miss your services. Are you thinking about staying in Philadelphia?"

"No, I can't seem to take this cold anymore, I'm heading for Florida."

I replied, "I hope I can do as good a job as you have all these years."

"You know something Ray; I had this same conversation with my boss 40 years ago. You'll be fine."

Getting to my office, I checked my calendar, and I was free Wednesday night. I had Sue's phone number in my rolodex file and called. The switch board operator connected me to her office, "Eastern Banking Services, can I help you?"

"Sue, It's Ray. I'm free Wednesday evening. What time shall I pick you up?"

"I get done work at 4:30. It'll take me about an hour to get home."

I interrupted, "Why don't I pick you up where you work and drive you home? Where's your office?"

"It's at 15th and Walnut Street, The Korn Exchange Building."

"Whoa! That's a bank for high rollers," I said.

"That's right. You have to be a depositor with at least $500,000."

"I'm glad our having to meet, didn't depend on me being a depositor. If it was, we would have never met," I said.

"You can never tell. We might have met somewhere else. I'll see you Wednesday at 4:30 outside my building."

Losing myself in work for the next few days was easy. It was beginning to pile up. Wednesday at 4:30, I was outside her office building. Seeing my car double parked, she quickly hurried to it and got in. The traffic was heavy on the expressway and it took about 40 minutes to get to her home.

Getting out, she said, "I'll call Delores and tell her we'll be there about 6:30."

"That's fine. I'll come back and pick you up after I change. That way we won't have to take two cars."

"I'll see you then," she replied closing the door.

At 6:00 I was back and she was ready. "You look wonderful Sue. I like that outfit."

She was dressed in gray slacks with a cream colored pearl blouse, complemented by a blue sapphire necklace. I had dressed casual with dungarees and a bulky knit sweater, the way I would normally dress going to Don's, but looking at her, I felt a little inferior saying, "I'm sorry Sue, but the way you're dressed, makes me feel ashamed I didn't think about getting dressed up. It wasn't very thoughtful of me. Usually, when I go to Don's, we're sort of lounge buddies."

"That's alright. I never thought I'd make you feel uncomfortable, but I assumed knowing Delores, she would make this a candle light dinner for the four of us."

"That sounds amorous, maybe I should drift back to my apartment and change?"

Looking at me to pass on my embarrassment, she replied, "I don't think so, you're fine."

Countering her statement to correct my mistake, I said, "No, I insist. Delores is making my favorite, spaghetti. I think that warrants me being formal."

Getting back to my apartment, I said, "Wait here, I'll be right back."

It only took 10 minutes to change then return, and I felt better that we looked equally dressed. Arriving at Don's, Sue's intuition was spot on. The table was set with candles to add to the mood.

Delores was bound to the fact I wasn't comfortable with my life style, and forcefully wanted to change it by playing cupid several times before with other friends of hers.

"Delores, I have to confess, Sue was right. She said it would be a candle lit dinner. After seeing the way she was dressed, it embarrassed me to the point I went back home and changed. I'm glad I did. Even Don's dressed a little better than casual."

Delores went right by my statement. Looking at Sue she asked, "That's a great looking outfit Sue. Where did you get it?"

"Sachs, on Chestnut Street," Sue replied.

"Why don't you come in the kitchen and help me with the hors d'oeuvres? You can tell me all about the weekend."

Hearing that remark from Delores, I looked over my shoulder. I assumed they weren't only going to discuss what happened at the séance, the conversation was going to be about whether Sue and I would possibly have a relationship, and I think she realized it, giving me a nod confirming my suspicions. After a few minutes, they returned to the living room.

I said, "Delores you went to an awful lot of trouble setting the mood with the candles, it's just like a séance. Should I go back up and borrow the blue bottle from George?" everyone laughed.

She replied, "No, but from what Sue told me, I'm pissed that I wasn't there. I never suspected there would be a resolve with Adda's presence. I'm glad she finally found peace," throwing in a dig she continued, "Now Sue won't have to worry about two women in the kitchen."

Sue looked a little embarrassed with the remark, but didn't disapprove. She looked at me as though she was expecting me to have a response, but instead, I smiled, changing the subject.

"When's the dinner ready?" I asked.

"It's ready now. Why don't the three of you sit down, I'll get it."

Sue quickly added, "I'll help."

I thought Sue volunteered to have the opportunity to tell Delores to back off from pushing us together. Sue already knew the interest was there on my part, but didn't want to rush things. I must have been right, after returning to the dining room, I could sense they seemed to have a different attitude.

"The dinner smells great Delores. You're one hell of a cook, especially when it comes to Italian food."

Sue replied, "I tasted her Italian dinners before. They are great."

Don poured the wine and we toasted my success of getting rid of all the spirits from my house.

During the conversation at dinner I said, "Don, I forgot to tell you,

Mr. Johnson's retiring in the spring. He told me he's referring me to corporate headquarters as his replacement."

"That's great, congratulations. I guess you already figured it out, you won't be able to take off on Fridays as you've been doing."

"You know, I never thought of that. I guess I'll have to restrict my trips to when I have a long holiday weekend. I think the pay increase will be worth it though. Maybe I can hire a contractor up there to do some of the work for me, just to get ahead of the game."

"That's an idea. This way all you have to do is go up on weekends and check the progress."

Delores, impatient with our conversation interrupted, "Now, how about telling me about the weekend?"

"I thought Sue would have told you by now," I replied.

"No, she insisted that you two should be here to tell me. She didn't want to leave anything out."

I looked at Sue waiting for her to begin the conversation, but when she didn't, I prompted her, "Well, Sue, go ahead."

I enjoyed my meal while listening to her relate the weekend. She didn't miss anything, for the exception of not telling Delores about looking into the blue bottle and seeing a mist that I couldn't see. The conversation sort of drifted in the direction of George's deteriorating condition, and the concern from Delores and Don was obvious.

"That's a shame he doesn't move in with someone until his times up," Don said.

Delores looked at him with a cold stare replying, "That's a terrible statement- 'until his time is up.' then looked at me asking, "Ray, I wonder if there's anyone that can move in with him," looking at Don with a sneer, she gave him back his own words, "You know, until his times up."

I replied, "I think that's what June and Frank are working on. The trouble is everyone he knows or knows him, still work full time jobs. They would have to be there from the time they get off work, until they go back in the morning. Who'll watch him during the day?"

Sue replied, "Maybe they can get two or three people that can alternate schedules. This way, the only problem would be finding someone that can stay overnight." Sadly continuing as she ran her finger around the edge of her wine glass, "In his condition, I don't think he'll last very long."

"I wouldn't mind seeing the old man again. Don, maybe we can take a ride up this weekend ourselves?" Delores suggested.

"I won't have a problem with that. Let's see what the weather's going to be," he replied.

Delores seemed happy with his commitment, and the rest of the dinner conversation was scattered with other subjects.

One of my comments was directed at Delores, "You know, if it wasn't for you introducing me to Sue, I may not have ever met her, especially if it depended on meeting her where she works."

Don began to remark, "That's where she met her husb___." He never had a chance to finish, and I'm sure his statement was interrupted by a nudge under the table by Delores' foot. Sue finished Don's statement, "Yes, that's where I met my ex."

Sensing a little tension in her voice, I tried adding a little humor with a reply, "Well I'm glad he decided to withdraw his money."

It was a vain attempt to smooth over an uncomfortable statement, and I know the forced laughter from Don and Delores was canned. Like viewers of a television comedy show, prompted to laugh at a particular scene, by laughter from the producers.

After dinner, Don and I retired to the living room, while Sue helped Delores clear the table. Before they joined us, Don said, "I sort of put my foot in my mouth at the table."

"We haven't discussed our married lives yet, but she did tell me that's where they met. I was giving her the opportunity to open up first. Was her ex wealthy?" I asked.

"Yes, very. Suppose you call me tomorrow night and I'll tell you what I know."

Looking surprised that he may have something awkward to talk about, I told him I'd call him at 7:00.

Within a few minutes the girls re-set the table with dessert. Delores announced, "Come on Don, Ray, the coffee and desserts on the table."

"And it looks scrumptious. Delores baked the pie herself," Sue added.

Don put his arms around Delores, and kissed the side of her neck, "I sure am lucky to have her," he said.

Delores gently pulled away, looking over her shoulder at him with a smile, "You only married me because I can cook."

We laughed then sat down.

Sue was right- the apple pie was two inches thick, with a light brown crust. Cutting into it released a little steam, and the aroma would make any hardened dieter abandon their principles.

"Looks great, Delores," I said, "I'll bet it tastes just as good."

The first bite reinforced my claim, it was delicious.

Looking at my watch, I was surprised it was already 9:00. "Delores, Don, thanks for a great dinner. We have to be going."

Sue added as she hugged Delores, "Thanks Dee, I'll have to return the favor," then hugged Don.

On the drive home, she broke the silence, "If we can get together some night this week, I'll tell you about my ex, it wasn't an easy divorce."

"Don't think you have to tell me because Don prompted the conversation. Whenever you're comfortable enough to talk about it, is fine with me. I was sure Delores must have kicked Don's leg, when he blurted it out."

She laughed, "Yeah, I know, she told me while we were in the kitchen."

She became serious for a moment as though she wanted to tell me something, but didn't quite know how to begin. "You know Ray, while I was in the kitchen with Delores, I had the strangest feeling."

"What was that?"

She looked at me with sadness in her eyes and said, "I had the feeling that George was trying to contact me."

Now she had me become serious, "You mean like he was trying to contact you psychically?"

"Yes, the urge to see him was extremely strong. More so than any other experience I've ever had."

Focusing my undivided attention, I asked, "What do you think it means?"

"I don't know, but I wouldn't put off going back to see him too long. I have the feeling he won't be with us much longer."

"Then we'll make it this weekend. Delores planned on that anyway. I'll give Don a call."

Pulling into her driveway, I put the car in park then looked at her. Her eyes seem to have a sparkle from the motion detector flood lights shining on the driveway, and I drew her close kissing her. The kiss was a much more passionate one than the last time, and I knew my feelings were becoming stronger, and hoped hers were too.

Chapter 4

I went home to my apartment Thursday evening, to see the light blinking on my answering machine and hit the play back button. It was a message from Frank. The first thought that ran through my mind was, did it have something to do with the house? Quickly returning the call, June answered the phone.

"Hello. Who's calling?"

"June, this is Ray, your new neighbor. Frank left a message. What did he want?"

"Ray, he just wanted to tell you George passed away."

I expected he was on his death bed, but remembering the last few words of conversation with Sue, sent a chill up my spine. Did he really contact her spiritually as he was dying?

I asked, "June was it last night?"

"Yes, how did you know?"

I went silent for a few moments, then asked, "June, do you know about what time it was?"

She replied, "Me and Frank were at his house around 8:30 last night. He was lying on the sofa when we came in. I went over to ask him if he needed anything, and he opened his eyes and said," pausing, as if she was hesitant to repeat his words.

I became impatient waiting for her answer, and said, "Well, what did he say?"

She couldn't know why I was so intent on finding out what time it was, and I apologized, "I'm sorry June for asking so abruptly, but it's important."

"When I shook him, he looked up at us and said Sue for some reason. It was around 8:30."

Her words sent an immediate chill up my spine, and I felt the hair on the back of my neck rise. Was it a coincidence that Sue had the strongest urge to see him as he was dying? Remembering the serious look on her face, I don't think it was a coincidence. It was a real psychic connection.

"June, what are the funeral arrangements?" I asked.

"They're scheduled for this Saturday. If you're coming up, you better bring a U-Haul trailer."

"Why's that?"

"It looked as though his last thoughts were about Sue. He looked up at me then smiled. He must have been content. He had a paper in his hand that will's his great grandmother's bureau and bench seat, along with the blue bottle we used for the séances, to Susan."

Those words sent another chill up my spine. Having the paper in his hand, could his last thoughts have been about Sue getting the dresser-ensuring in some way that whatever spirit has a connection to it would survive. The fact that she's a psychic, is that the reason he was smiling? I didn't need another episode with her being possessed by a spirit. Temporarily forgetting June was still on the line, she asked again, "Will you be coming up this weekend?"

It snapped me back to our conversation. "Believe it or not June, we were at Delores and Don's for dinner last night, and talked about coming up this weekend. I guess with George dying, that will confirm our plans. I know I want to make the funeral, and I'm sure everyone else does too. We'll probably get there sometime late Friday evening. I don't think anyone would be able to take off work tomorrow on such a short notice. We'll leave after work."

She replied, "I'll see you Saturday then. Be careful driving, it's supposed to rain, but up here, a shift in the wind, can make a weatherman a liar."

I hung up the phone and stood for a few minutes looking at it. I wondered whether I should even call Sue. If I did, how was I going to tell her? I decided to call Don first, and dialed his number.

Don answered, "Hello who's calling?"

"Don, this is Ray. I just got a call from June- Frank's wife. George died last evening. The funeral's set for Saturday. I don't know whether you still have plans to go, but I'm going. I intend to leave tomorrow afternoon after work. I won't be able to take off the whole day on short notice, but I might be able to get out of the office a little earlier. How about you?"

"Delores and I are a definite. I think I may be able to get off earlier too. I'll give you a call at your office in the morning. Delores doesn't have anything planned. She's been looking forward to the trip since we discussed it. How about Susan?"

"I haven't called her yet. I was thinking about not telling her at all."

"Why not?"

"I didn't tell you, but she said she had an episode while she was in the kitchen at your house."

"What was that?" he asked.

"After I got her home, she told me about having the strongest urge to see George."

"What's so strange about that? We were all discussing him."

"I know, but according to June, it was about the same time he died. Not only that, June told me when she found him, he had a paper in his hand willing the dresser and bench along with the blue bottle to Susan."

"Why Susan, doesn't he have any relatives to give it to?"

"No. He told us that when we last visited. He was adamant Sue should take it, and had her write out a paper claiming the dresser, and signed it. I'll have to get a trailer while we're there, since you're going, you can help me load it."

"That's not a problem. If I were you, I would think about not wanting to include Susan. I know that would really bother her. Why don't you just suggest her not going?"

"Maybe you're right. I'll give her a call now. Call me tomorrow to firm up our plans."

It took me a few moments after I hung up talking to Don, wondering how I was going to present it to Sue. At best, I knew she would be angry. Should I just do as Don suggested and not try to talk her out of going? I thought to myself, "Alright coward, here goes." After dialing her number, the phone rang twice before she answered.

"I know Ray- its bad news about George isn't it?"

This was getting weird. It's the second time she could read my thoughts, and not being in the same room, or within several blocks of each other, really unsettled my nerves.

"Yes, Sue, he died. I spoke to June a little while ago. She told me when she found him- he had the paper in his hand you made out for the dresser and bench seat. Apparently he must have been thinking about it before he passed away."

She asked quietly, "Ray, did she say when he died?"

I hesitated to answer, not wanting to make more of the coincidences that were already present, so I lied, "No, I didn't ask; and she didn't say. I already spoke to Don, and like myself, will try getting off early tomorrow afternoon. I'll probably be ready to hit the road by 3:00 p.m. Do you think you'll be ready?"

"Yes, in fact, I'm already half packed. I started after you dropped me off."

"Was it just in preparation for the weekend, or a premonition you had?" I asked.

"I never gave it a thought until now. It must have been a premonition. I've already packed a black dress. Normally I would have never done that. Pick me up as soon as you can, I'll be waiting."

***

The next day just before noon, I received a call from Don, "Ray, I'm getting ready to leave my office. How about you?"

I swung around in my chair and looked up at the clock.

"Don, I'll be leaving in about 15 minutes. I'm already packed and so is Sue." I was interrupted by him asking, "So you couldn't talk her out of not going?"

"No, I didn't try. I'm glad I didn't. When I called last night, she already knew George had died."

"You didn't mention to her about the coincidence of him dying at the same time of her premonition with him did you?" he asked.

"No, and I'd appreciate it if you or Delores didn't say anything either."

"I won't. I never discussed it with Delores, so there's no problem there."

"Good, I'll see you at your place about 3:00."

Leaving work, I hurriedly picked up Sue then headed for Don's. They were waiting at the curb when I pulled up.

"Hi Delores, Don. I'm glad we can leave earlier. I don't like the looks of those rain clouds."

Delores replied, "Maybe it will hold off until we get there."

"I hope so," I replied.

The drive up was scattered conversation of things we did and saw with Old George. Delores asked, "Sue, I understand he left the dresser and bench seat, along with the blue bottle for you in his will. Why did he do that?"

"I don't really know. He said he had no relatives and wanted to give it to me."

After a few minutes of silence, I sensed a little resentment on Delores's part. I think it bothered her not being considered first, and I guess it was because she knew George a little longer.

After stopping for dinner, we continued to Frank and June's. Arriving at their driveway, the outside light came on. They were apparently awaiting our arrival to tell us about the arrangements that were made for the funeral. The porch door swung open as we walked to the house and Frank stepped out.

"Good evening, come in. June will put on the coffee."

Following him into the house, we acknowledged June's thoughtfulness with her offer.

"Frank, I'm really sorry for not being able to see George at least once more before he died. I really took a liking to that old man," Don said.

Delores added, "He was such a darling old soul, it makes me sad. One good thing though, we have a chance to see him before he's buried. Where is the viewing being held?"

"The viewing is in town at the Stewart Funeral parlor, 10:00 to noon. It's on Elm Street right off of Main. The cemetery is the one on Main Street. I believe that's where his mother and grandmother are buried. I don't believe they'll be very many people at the funeral parlor. Everyone he knew, are probably already dead, except for the few that had dealings with him."

Frank chimed in, "June, I'm glad you added, 'Except for the few that had dealings with him." June gave him a nudge to the ribs to return him to being serious about the funeral arrangements.

Finishing our coffee, Sue remarked, "We'll be there at 10:00. We can't stay here too long, we haven't checked into a motel yet."

Getting up to leave, Frank walked us to the door and kept the porch light on until we were in the car. After we pulled out onto the road, he flicked the light switch off and on several times to signal us goodnight.

Arriving at the motel we checked in. As we were standing in the hall just before entering our different rooms I said, "Good night all. It's been a long day and a long drive. I won't have any problems falling asleep tonight. Good night Sue."

"Good night, Ray. I hope I won't have any problem. I'm not looking forward to tomorrow. I've never been to a funeral."

Delores, Don and I paused for a moment and looked at her. I asked, "Are you serious, you've never been to a funeral?"

"No, this will be my first. Well, actually it's my second. When my grandfather died I was only 5 and don't remember it."

"Well, if you have any problem, I'll be right there."

Pushing the door to my room open, I said goodnight again then closed it behind me. The whole time getting ready for bed, I thought about what Sue said. She didn't mention her mother or father. I guess they're still alive. I climbed into bed and within a few minutes was fast asleep.

⁂

It seemed as though I just closed my eyes, and when I opened them, dawn was breaking. I dialed Sue's room and a tired sounding voice answered.

"Hello Ray, how did you sleep?"

"Like a baby. How about you?"

"I tossed and turned for awhile, but eventually fell asleep. I wonder if Delores and Don are awake."

"Why don't you give them a call? I'll take a quick shower and meet you in the dining room."

"Will do, I'm hungry this morning. We haven't had anything to eat since dinner last night."

"I know. I'll bet Don's already down there."

As I entered the cafeteria, Don gave me a wave and I returned the salutation in kind. He was already sitting at a table in the corner, with a plate full of waffles and a cup of coffee, and after retrieving my breakfast fare, I joined him.

"Don, I can't believe Sue's never been to a funeral."

Looking up from his plate he said, "That's not so strange, Delores hasn't either."

"You're kidding me!"

"No. I'm serious. I don't know, maybe it has something to do with their ability that makes them shun those kind of events. I have a sister that's deathly afraid of being in a hospital."

"That's understandable," I replied, "Most people don't like being in them."

Pausing for a moment looking at me over the fork full of food, he said, "I don't mean as a patient. I mean physically not wanting to be in there."

We were almost finished breakfast when the girls finally joined us. They were both dressed in black for the funeral, and Don and I were dressed in dark colored casual clothes. We talked about the funeral arrangements, and decided if the girls didn't want to see him, they could wait in the lobby of the funeral parlor. At 9:00 we left the motel.

The sky was overcast and walking to the car a light misty rain blew down on us.

"I should have thought to bring an umbrella," Sue said.

"I never thought of bringing one either," Delores said.

Waiting for the car to warm, I said, "It's befitting weather for George's funeral."

Delores remarked with a little hostility in her voice, "What do you mean? He doesn't deserve this crappy weather."

"Delores, I wasn't thinking along those lines. I was merely pointing out even the sky is weeping the passing of a great guy."

With that statement in my mind, I began to reflect on the initial meeting with George, the day Frank drove me to his house. Seeing him sitting on the back porch sorting apples from his trees, the conversation that exposed an unintentional home spun humor, coupled with years of experience in life. The immediate offer to help a total stranger, made his character complete. As genuine a person someone would meet in their life, one would carry his memory as long as they lived.

Within the hour, we pulled up in front of the funeral parlor. There were only two other vehicles in the small parking lot, one I identified as Frank's pickup truck, and the other I didn't recognize. Going inside, Frank and June greeted us at the door. It was as solemn as every funeral parlor I've ever been in. Passing through the doorway to the casket, brings a feeling of reverence. The standing pole lights at each end of the casket with funnel shaped globes, accented a muted illumination of the deceased lying in state. It's as if they were only sleeping, but somehow realizing they were dead, one gets the feeling they know you're there.

Holding Susan's hand, we entered the room. I could feel her palm grow cold and she began to shake as we approached the casket.

"Are you alright? You look a little pale?" I asked.

She slowly looked up at me but didn't answer. I could feel her palm sweating and the trembling became stronger.

"Susan, I think you should just wait in the lobby."

"No, I want to go through with this," she said.

Looking at George lying there, it was as if he was sleeping. He wasn't dressed in a suit as most traditional viewings, but in a green plaid flannel shirt buttoned at the top, and khaki pants. It was the way I saw him when we first met, casual, comfortable to him. It fit with his personality, and I believe he would have wanted it that way. We stood alongside the casket and Sue began to cry. I tried leading her away, but she pulled back. Staring at his face becoming more distraught, I had to overpower her forcing her to leave the room.

I sat her down in the lobby and got her a drink of water. Delores had a similar affect, but not as strong.

"Sue, I think this was a bad idea. Are you sure you're alright to continue, or shall I take you back to the motel?" I said.

June remarked, "Susan, you can go to our house to wait until we get there. You'll probably feel more comfortable."

"No, I'll be fine," she replied.

I asked, "June, I see another car in the parking lot, is that a friend or relative?"

"He's a long time friend but he's also a local lawyer. Mr. Brown and George go back about 80 years."

As we were standing in the lobby, he approached us, and June introduced me.

"Jerry, this is Ray Bishop. He bought Frank's mother and father's farm."

"Pleased to meet you." he said as he stretched out his fragile hand. He was short with small features, a pretty good match in physical appearance as George, except for an upper spinal problem, which made him slightly hunchback. He was dressed in a dark suit with a white shirt and dark blue bowtie, traditional for a lawyer of his time.

"Mr. Bishop, June found a paper in George's hand when they discovered his body. It was a hand written note willing George's great grandmother's dressing bureau, bench seat, and a blue bottle to a woman by the name of Susan Heart. It's not written in George's penmanship, but I recognize his signature. Do you know anything about this?"

"Yes, I do. June can verify the fact he wanted to will it to the woman sitting in the lobby, she's Susan Heart. I was there when he told her to make out the paper for him to sign."

Frank, who was speaking with Ed Jones, another friend of George's who came to the viewing, entered our conversation. Overhearing what June said, Frank confirmed it. Jerry stretched out his hand again saying, "Well, it was nice making your acquaintance. I hope to see you again soon. Frank has the key to George's. He can let you in to get the dresser whenever you get a chance."

"Thank you Mr. Brown," I replied.

"No, just call me Jerry," he said, as he put on his coat.

"Ok, Jerry. I'll be looking forward to seeing you in the future."

After he left I asked, "Frank, I'll have to rent some sort of small trailer to get the dresser back to the city. Do you know where I can get one?"

"There's a U-Haul Rental at a local gas station in town. They should have what you need," he said.

"Thanks! I'll stop after we leave here. I don't want to stay much longer. Susan's having a hard time with this."

"Yes, I notice, maybe that's a good idea. June and me are going to the cemetery. Will you?"

"I'd like to keep her from going, but I don't think she'll listen. Let me ask."

Susan was sitting in the lobby having a conversation with Delores, occasionally wiping tears from her eyes. I asked, "Sue, do you want to leave, and go someplace where we can have a coffee? I don't think you should go to the cemetery."

Her face took on the same resentful look she gave me when I tried to talk her out of coming. With everything that's happened, I was sorry I ever mentioned it. I asked, "Why the black look? It was only a suggestion."

Her angry look turned into something approximating a smile, "I know you're concerned with me Ray, but I'm fine."

"Ok, if you insist."

Delores added, "We'll be fine Ray. I understand what she's going through. It's not easy for me either. We have an extra sense most other people don't have, but we'll be fine."

Don looked at me, and motioned with his head for me to join him outside.

"Ray, I would have never brought those two along if I knew this was going to happen."

"I know, Don, I tried to suggest it to Sue, but she gave me such a hateful look. It's too late now. I'll have to go through with it."

"You say a hateful look?" he inquired.

"Yes, after I agreed to let her come, she changed 180 degrees as if I never suggested for her to stay home."

Don replied, "That's weird. I never knew her to have a bad attitude, even going through her divorce. It was a real dog fight."

"Well, maybe we're looking at it wrong," I suggested, "We'll see. Oh, by the way. Frank told me there's a gas station in town that rents U-Haul trailers. When we leave the cemetery, we can swing by and get one, then pick up the dresser." Looking at the sky I continued, "The rain seems to have stopped. Maybe Frank can loan me a tarp and some rope to lash the dresser down, just in case."

Don replied, "I'm sure he will. Maybe he can help us load it too. I'll ask."

The procession was scant going to the cemetery, only four vehicles. It was bothering Susan more than the rest of us, and I was hoping the graveside interment would be short. The minister that performed it wasn't familiar with George- he wasn't a church going person. As everyone began walking back to their cars, Susan stopped, then placed her hand on the casket as a parting gesture.

"Come on Sue," I said, "We have to pick up a trailer and canvas at Frank's to carry the dresser back to the city."

She looked at me then looked back at the casket, as I was leading her away.

June said, "Frank, why don't you go with Ray and Don to get the trailer and pick up the dresser? I'll take Delores and Sue to the house for lunch. After you're through, you can come get the girls then they can head back to the city."

Frank replied, "Ok, we'll see you later."

Arriving at the gas station, the owner was locking the door. Luckily Frank knew him and asked. "Ralph, are we to late to rent a trailer?"

"Hello, Frank," looking up at the clock in the front window. "In a few more minutes you would have been. How did the funeral go for old George?"

"Well, there wasn't many people there. I guess most everybody he knows, have already passed away."

"Yeah, I'm sorry I couldn't make it. My helper didn't show up today. I guess he was out late last night. You know how these young kids are, no responsibility."

"Yep, not like when we were kids," Frank replied.

I thought it amusing that every generation looks back on their past as though they never entertained the thought of staying out late.

After hooking up the trailer, we headed for George's. After backing the trailer up to the porch, I suddenly felt solemn. We were about to take a lifelong possession of one of the nicest people I've ever met. I thought, "If George is able to know our presence, I hope he'd be smiling at us for insuring the dresser's safe future."

Frank unlocked the door and we went in. The house had a strange feeling of being empty, and the chill inside was appropriate for the occasion. Going into the bedroom, the dresser was the most prominent piece of furniture. It was about 5 feet wide with a large mirror framed in beautifully carved wood, flanked by mirrors that were smaller, but set on a slight angle, to give the user a side view of their face. It was low to the floor, suitable for a woman to sit at, applying whatever makeup or brushing out her hair. There were two small doors on each side with a shallow drawer in the center. The surface had a unique half round extension from the base of the mirror with a lid that swung up-probably used for storing hair brushes and combs, or possibly jewelry. The cushioned bench seat that was part of the set, had ornately carved legs with a beautifully carved low back, and I knew it must have cost quite a sum of money when it was purchased.

When I lifted the lid of the center piece, there was a towel wrapped around something. After unwrapping it, I saw it was the blue bottle from the séances. Carefully picking it up, I went to the window. Rolling up the shade, I held it up to the light coming through the window. I wasn't able to see the mist Sue said she saw, other than being convoluted, it was perfectly clear. I looked around to find something heavier to wrap it in so it wouldn't get broken during the move. To insure its safety, I put it back in the compartment and used several more towels to pack around it.

When Don and Frank entered the room, Frank asked, "Do you think we should take the mirror off to transport it?"

I replied, "I don't think so. I looked at the back and it's built pretty solid. I'd be afraid to damage it. If we rope it off real good, it shouldn't be a problem."

"Ok, you're the boss," he replied.

Picking up each end, we carefully loaded the precious cargo, covered it with canvas, and securely roped it in. I went back for the bench seat and took one last look around the room. I spied a picture on an end table of George when he was about 10- standing next to who I assumed was his grandmother, and asked, "Frank, do you think anyone would mind if I take this picture of George?"

He replied, "I don't think anyone would mind. I don't know what's going to happen to all the other little things here." surveying the room, motioning with his hand as he spoke.

I picked up the photo and paused to look at it. After eyeing the room one last time, we left the house. After returning to Frank's to pick up the girl's, we bid Frank and June adieu- then left for the city.

On the ride home, we stopped several times on Susan's command, to look at the precious cargo to make sure it was still secure. Susan got out of the car each time to personally supervise, tugging at the ropes that secured it, making sure there was no room for error. Satisfied it was safe enough to continue, she got back in the car.

Chapter 5

Arriving at Sue's, we backed into the driveway and unloaded the cargo. I asked, "Sue, where do you want this?"

"If you don't mind, first take the dresser I have in the bedroom, and put it here in the garage. I want this one put in its place."

"You're the boss," replied Don.

Taking the one that was there, I commented, "Don, this looks brand new. Why does she want to change it?"

"That's what I thought when we walked in. I wonder what she's going to do with it."

Just then, Sue entered the room with Delores. Overhearing us, she remarked, "I'm going to sell it."

Delores replied, "Why would you want to do that? It looks brand new."

"It is. I bought it to replace the one my ex and I had. I didn't want any mementos of anything that had to do with our marriage."

Don and I looked at each other. I remembered him telling me their divorce was a real dog fight, so I chose not to comment, and I think Delores and Don thought likewise. After changing places with the one we brought from George's, we covered the new one we put in the garage with the tarp from the trip.

Don said, "Delores, we have to drop off the trailer. Why don't you wait here? We shouldn't be very long."

"Ok, I'll help Sue," running her hand over the dresser. "This could use a good going over with furniture polish. Sue do you have any?"

"Yes, I'll get a couple of soft cloths too."

Within the hour, we returned. I said goodbye to Sue, then drove Delores and Don home. On the way, Delores commented, "Ray, something seems strange."

"What seems strange?" I asked.

"The attachment Sue has with that dressing bureau, it isn't normal. When we were polishing it, I was talking to her, but she seemed as though she either didn't hear me, or was ignoring my question. She began quietly humming as a mother would do with a baby, really weird."

"What kind of question were you asking?"

"I made a comment about the blue bottle, and why George willed it to her."

"What did she say?"

"She kept humming quietly as she took the bottle from the towels wrapped around it. She put it in front of her on the dresser and stared at it for a few minutes. I asked if she was ok, and she replied staring at me, 'Delores, do you see anything in the bottle?' When I picked it up at George's, I thought it was just a residue that was on the inside and needed to be cleaned."

"Well, was it?"

Delores hesitated to answer, seemingly deep in thought, then replied, "Well, when I looked after she cleaned it, I couldn't see anything. The bottle was clear, but she said she could still see a mist. I'm beginning to wonder whether you should have left it at George's."

I didn't reflect on her comment, but thought she may have been right. Maybe I should have left it there.

Pulling up to their house I said, "Well, goodbye guys, I'll give you a call later this week. Maybe we can get together for dinner at Sue's. That is, if I can get her to agree."

Don replied, "Call me Tuesday and let us know."

"That's a bet. I'll do that."

On the way home, I couldn't stop thinking about what Delores said. That, coupled with Sue's strange reactions on several occasions, made me pull to the curb. I thought, "Should I go to her house and make sure she's alright?" My second thought told me to go home instead then call her. I pulled out in traffic again, and within a few blocks, I was at my apartment building. Hurrying up the stairs, I could hear the phone ringing as I unlocked the door. Quickly grabbing it, I was hoping it was Susan.

"Hello! Sue?"

"Yes, Ray, it's me."

"That's a relief."

"What's a relief?"

"I was worried about you."

"Why? I'm fine. You just left here a half hour ago."

"I know, but with the way you acted a few times during the weekend, I wasn't sure whether it was too much of a strain on you. For someone that hadn't had that many encounters with George, your reaction to his funeral didn't seem like it was warranted."

"No, you're wrong, it did warrant it. I have an inner soul that sometimes reacts to certain people. It's something I've experienced before. Not often, but sometimes it happens."

I could hear her moving about as we were speaking, and she suddenly dropped the phone.

"Sue, are you there?"

"Yes, I'm still here. I dropped the phone."

"What are you doing?"

"I'm trying to wipe the mirror of the dressing table. It has a lot of finger prints from moving it."

I quickly replied, "Can't it wait until we finish our conversation?"

"I'm sorry, you're right, go ahead. What were we talking about?"

"You were telling me about having an inner soul that reacts to certain people, remember?"

"Oh, yes. Well that's about all. For some reason it just happens."

I replied, "Oh, I almost forgot. Don wanted to know if we could get together for dinner later this week. He said if we are, I'm supposed to call him Tuesday evening. I think he was hinting to have it at your house.

"I'll have to check my schedule, but it should be fine for Wednesday or Thursday. I'll let you know," she replied.

"Whatever day you decide will be fine, as long as you make the dinner."

After a few moments of silence, I asked, "Sue, are you still there?"

"Yes, I'm still here. Who's suggestion was that? Yours?" she asked.

I laughed, "No, it was actually Don's, but I think Delores was part of the plot."

"Well if they asked, it'll have to be here. As I said, I think it will be fine for Wednesday or Thursday. It won't be hard to figure out what to make for dinner, they both love my lasagna."

"That's great, so do I. I'll call you tomorrow to firm things up."

It seemed as though she was hurrying me off the phone for some reason, and wondered why, but didn't comment.

After cleaning the mirror, Susan sat down on the bench seat, and opened the doors of the small end cabinets. They were empty, and she wiped them clean, before transferring her beauty items from the bureau she was getting rid of. After completing the task, she tried to pull open the center drawer to remove it. It opened part way, and appeared to be stuck. She pulled on the handles a little harder, but it was no use, it wouldn't budge. Getting up from the bench seat, she knelt on the floor to get a better look. Realizing something was stuck in the rear of the dust cover preventing the drawer from opening, she put her hand in as far as she could reach. She didn't see anything inside the drawer, but felt something in back of it. It felt like paper but stiffer. As hard as she tried, she couldn't remove it.

Getting a flashlight, she shined it on the object. It wasn't paper. It felt more like parchment. Something she'd seen before. She had seen a few old documents like it where she worked. Pushing a little harder, she was able to move it down. Gently pulling on the drawer, it finally opened all the way. Gingerly lifting it from its track, she laid it on the floor. Looking into the empty space, she retrieved a small brown folder lying between the bottom of the drawer, and the dust cover beneath it. That's what was preventing the drawer from opening.

Taking it out, she could see it was a few parchment pages in a brown leather folder, bound together with leather thongs. By its appearance, she knew it had to be quite old. One corner was dog eared from being stuck, but other than that, it seemed to be intact. Carefully dusting the outside cover, she laid it aside. Checking to see if there was anything else in the open space, she dusted the drawer and returned it to the bureau.

Still sitting on the floor with her legs crossed, she opened the folder and began to read its contents. The words looked as though they were written with a quill pen, and the pages had darkened considerably with age, but were still legible.

The words were a mixture of short sentences, with what appeared to be responses as if they were recited in a group type environment. Getting up and sitting on the bench, she put the open folder in front of her and began to read the words. They didn't seem to make much sense, but she was astonished when she noticed as she read, the blue bottle began to brighten. She picked it up thinking the lighting in the room was somehow reflecting differently, causing it to appear brighter. No, nothing changed. With a few moments of silence, she noticed the bottle began to grow dim once again.

When she continued to read, the bottle began to get brighter. Shocked at her discovery, she realized the bottle was being controlled by the words she was reading. Quickly putting it down, she went to the kitchen for a drink of water. Pouring it from the pitcher, she noticed her hand shaking. With all the séances she had ever been involved with, she never had this kind of experience. The only time it came close, was her first weekend at the farm, when the spirit entered her body before she was prepared. She thought, "Should I continue? Why not? I'm safe in my own home."

Returning to the dressing mirror, she picked up the bottle once again. It still had a mist within it, and she continued reading the words from the ancient text she discovered, but did not understand.

"Arawn- Brigid- Cernuvnos- Cerridwin- Danu, Herne- Liugh- Morgan- Rhiannon, Taranis."

With each word, the bottle became brighter. Looking closer at the mist, she could see a woman brushing out her long blond hair. Suddenly, she slowly turned as if she could see Susan. As the image became clearer, Susan quickly sat back, and turned to see if there was anyone else in the room. Frightfully, she realized the image being projected, was by the blue bottle. Was it a mirage? Carefully watching the image become clearer, Susan was shocked to see the woman's face. She was old and wrinkled, but her hair wasn't white as it should have been. It was blond, the color of a much younger woman.

Looking at the mist, she began to see a young boy sitting on the floor coming into view. Suddenly she recalled George's exact words, 'I would sometimes sit on the floor with my legs crossed, watching my grandmother brushing out her long hair. She was reciting strange words I didn't understand, and for some strange reason, her hair never turned gray, like an older persons hair should have.'

Sue obviously stumbled upon the text George's grandmother was reading from. What did it all mean? Could the young boy coming into view, be George when he was a small boy? How was the bottle able to project the past?

Somehow, the bottle had more mystical power than even George knew, and Sue had more questions than answers. Instead of being afraid, which should have been a normal reaction, it made her more curious, of whatever mystical powers the bottle possessed, sharing its secret with no one else. Continuing to read the words from the text, she could see faint images coming into view. Like turning back the pages of history, it led her to the American Civil War, and the image of a Confederate soldier dying on a battlefield. Within a few moments, it was an image of a dead American Revolution War soldier, sitting on an old rocker, on the porch of a log cabin. There appeared to be an old woman sitting next to him in a rocking chair, reading from the very same text she found. The woman looked remarkably like the image of George's grandmother, with young George sitting on the floor beside her. But wait, it couldn't be. The wars were almost 90 years apart. Her hair was blond, but her face was wrinkled, it had to be someone else, possibly George's great grandmother.

Watching the mist in the bottle intently, Sue saw periods where the mist would clear showing her a scene, then become misty again. Each time it cleared then re-emerged again, it was further back in time. With every leap into the past, the old woman never changed.

In the most recent scene, Sue saw the Confederate soldier with blood on his tunic, rise from the chair on the front porch of the old woman's cabin, and go in.

The old woman closed the text uttering a few more words then followed him. When the mist returned temporarily clearing, she saw an identical scene, but this time, it was a Revolutionary War soldier. He too had blood on his shirt. Afraid of what she was able to see, she quickly put down the bottle.

The grandfather's clock in the hall began to chime, and vibrated 11 times.

Looking up from the bottle, she hadn't realized the time had gone by so quickly. Opening the half round top of the desk, she carefully placed the bottle inside, and prepared for bed.

***

She was awoken in the morning by the sound of her alarm clock. Sitting up, she rubbed her eyes, wondering whether she dreamt the events of the evening before. Looking at the bureau she suddenly froze. The blue bottle wasn't in the hair brush drawer where she put it before she got ready for bed. It was standing upright on top of the lid. She distinctly remembered putting it away, and it shook her to the degree she entertained the thought of throwing it in the Schuylkill River on the way to work. Keeping a wary eye on the bottle while she dressed, she contemplated the thought.

Putting on her coat, she realized if she wanted to throw it away, she would have to drive to work, instead of taking public transportation which she normally did. She thought, 'Na, I'll leave it alone for now.' Closing the front door, she locked it then headed for work.

The day was moving at a fast pace, and she forgot the events of the evening before. Suddenly, the phone rang. Looking at the clock, it was already 1:00.

"Hello, who's calling?" she asked.

"Sue, it's Ray. Have you made a decision on what day you wanted to invite Delores and Don for dinner?"

"Not really. I haven't had time to think about it. Suppose I call Delores tonight and firm it up?"

"That sounds good. Are you busy tonight? If you're not, maybe we can get together?"

There were a few moments of silence, then I repeated my words. "Sue, did you hear me?"

"Ray, I think I'll pass for tonight. I think I may be coming down with a sore throat. Maybe it's from standing out in the cold rain at the cemetery."

It was as though she just heard me for the first time, and became obvious she was trying to figure out an excuse for staying out of my company.

"Is there anything I can get you, possibly something from the drug store?"

"No, not really, I think I have everything I need at home."

"Did you drive to work this morning, or take public transportation?"

"I took public transportation, why?"

"Well, how about me picking you up and driving you home? You won't have to worry about standing on a corner waiting for a bus in this cold. We're supposed to have flurries this afternoon."

"I'll be fine. Suppose I call you at 7:00?" she said.

Not wanting to push the issue, I replied, "I'll look forward to your call."

Seven o'clock rolled around, then 7:30, which quickly advanced to 8:00 p.m.

I decided to call, and the phone was picked up on the third ring.

"Sue, are you alright?"

She sounded distant, but replied, "Yes, I'm fine. What's wrong?"

"Nothing on my end, you were supposed to call me around 7:00 remember?"

"I must have dozed off. I took two cold tablets, sometimes they make me very tired. I'm sorry."

"That's ok, don't apologize. How's your sore throat?"

"I think if I take the day off tomorrow and just rest, I'll be fine."

"Are you sure you don't want me to get you anything?"

"No, I think I'll go and gargle again with peroxide. It seems to be helping. I'll call you at work tomorrow."

"Goodnight, Sue, take care of that sore throat."

"I will, and thanks for being concerned."

After hanging up, I stood for a moment looking at the phone. I thought, "It didn't sound like she just woke up. Is she blowing me off for some reason? I'll wait and see how she reacts when she calls me at work tomorrow."

I brought some insurance policies home to work on, but somehow couldn't get totally focused on them. For all intense and purposes, I should have left them at the office.

A strange feeling was coming over me about Sue and her relationship with the dressing bureau and the blue bottle. Could it be drawing her in by the power she feels, or is it more of my own imagination, being a rival to them? Oh well, I might just as well call it a night too. After getting a hot shower and sliding into bed, I was asleep in no time.

**

I woke in the morning with the same worries as the night before. They plagued my mind until I was at the insurance company. Before going into my office, I stood in the doorway watching people rushing back and forth from office to office on their daily routines. I never really noticed before, but all of a sudden, to me, it looked like organized chaos. I was amused by their action for a few moments, then entered my office.

Taking off my coat, I hung it in the closet and poured a freshly brewed cup of coffee. The aroma is always tempting, and a fresh cup is always welcomed, especially on a cold winter morning. Mr. Johnson, my boss, is always the first person in, and turns on the coffee maker. The last out of the company every day, he makes sure the pot is re-set for the following morning.

Within the hour, I picked up the receiver and thought I'd call Sue, but hesitated. I thought, "Should I bother?" Thinking I may be interrupting her sleep, I put down the phone.

Mr. Johnson slowly opened the door to my office and peeked in. Realizing I was alone, he said, "Ray, I have a policy here I'd like you to write. I know you've written policies for this firm before, and I know they'll appreciate someone they've worked with in the past."

Looking at the policy, I recognized the firm, "Sure thing Mr. Johnson, I'll get on it right away."

"How's that farm you bought?" he asked.

"It's fine. I went up this past weekend to a funeral. Other than that, it was pretty enjoyable. The person that died willed a dresser and a few items to a woman I'm seeing. Don and I brought them back to the city."

After a few moments, he asked, "Don: Would that be Don Lee who used to work here?"

"Yes, Mr. Johnson, we remained friends."

"I remember Don, he was a good employee. Where is he working now?"

It was a question I didn't want to answer. I didn't want him to know Don's working for a rival insurance firm, so I lied, "Well, he's in the banking industry now. I think he enjoys it a lot more."

Mr. Johnson replied, "I don't blame him. This insurance business is getting highly competitive. I'm glad I'm retiring in the spring. I hope you didn't mind me handing the reigns to you?"

"I hope I can do as good a job as you have all these years," I said.

Getting ready to leave the office, he looked over his shoulder replying, "I'm sure you will."

After making a few calls, I looked up at the clock. It was already 10:30, so I decided it wasn't too early to call Sue to ask how she was feeling. I dialed the number, and she picked up the phone on the second ring, "Good morning Ray."

Was it a coincidence, or the natural reply realizing I was concerned, and going to call?

"How are you feeling this morning?"

"I'm getting better. I'll call Delores this afternoon and make the arrangements for dinner."

"Don't do it unless you're sure you feel well enough."

"I'll make it for Thursday- how's that?" she replied.

"That's good for me. If you need anything call."

"I will Ray."

She hung up, and I went back to work feeling better she seemed to be recovering.

Looking over the policy request Mr. Johnson gave me, I delved into the finer points.

I called again just before lunch, but she didn't answer. I thought, "I'll try again later."

At 1 o'clock, I called again. This time she answered the phone with a less enthusiastic tone than this morning. I asked, "Did you contact Delores?"

"No I haven't," she replied.

"You sound tired, I'm sorry if I disturbed you."

"No. Thanks for calling. I should force myself to get out of bed."

Just then, there was a knock at my office door. It was my secretary telling me a high end client wanted to speak with me.

"Sue, I have to go, I have a client waiting. I'll call you tonight."

"Ok, I'll call Delores later," she replied.

As she lay there trying to get up enough energy to get out of bed, Susan realized she wouldn't be successful until her feet were actually on the floor. Standing there, scanning the room for her robe, she saw it draped over the chair at the dressing bureau. After putting it on, she sat down. All of a sudden she felt weak.

Normally, she would go to the shower first, but for some strange reason she abandoned her normal routine, and began brushing out her long hair. Her eyes focused on the folder for a few seconds, as if someone was beckoning her to open it. After taking it out, she opened it and began repeating the words she read last night. As she read, the bottle began to get brighter.

Picking it up, she could see the pages of history unfolding before her eyes again. Was it the history of mankind, or just the history of the blue bottle? Some scenes were what seemed to be private séances, while others appeared to be occult gatherings. For a moment she thought she recognized robed people congregated at Stonehenge, a formation of large pillars in England. Suddenly, the images stopped. She thought, "Is this what the mysterious mist is trying to show me? Is this the origin of the bottle's power?"

Seeking more information of what the bottle might be trying to communicate. She decided to get showered dressed, then go to the library for more information.

Upon her arrival, she asked the librarian, "Could you direct me to the section where I could obtain a book about Stonehenge?"

Giving Susan a strange look, she replied, "Come with me. If you're interested in the occult, we have a wide selection of books on the subject."

"Why would you think I'd be interested in the occult?"

"People that ask for that type of book, usually are. In fact, there are a few people that come here frequently and ask for them."

"Are you telling me they're people that belong to some sort of cult?"

"I don't know. They never talk about the subject. When I ask, they just smile and politely ignore my question, weird, just weird."

Getting to the proper section, she motioned with her hand, "Here's the section where you'll find what you're looking for."

"Thanks."

Scanning the books on the shelf, Susan realized there was quite a bit of information. Opening each one to examine it, she took a few then sat at one of the library tables. Checking the indexes, she put aside any book that went back farther than the 1600's. As she read, she never realized the significance of Stonehenge with people who were the educators of their time. The origin of the structure is unknown, but is believed to date back to 2,000 B.C. The vertical stones weighing more than 41 metric tons; are topped by stones almost as heavy. The site is aligned in the direction of the summer solstice, and bright stars in the position they would have been in *1500 BCE*. Historically, it was interesting, but Susan was looking for something more recent.

She found a book that had a picture of robed hooded people in a circle, with Stonehenge in the background. Stopping at that page, she was shocked at what she was seeing. She realized that was the period of history the bottle went back to. The picture was remarkably accurate to what the mist in the bottle showed. Taking it to the desk, she handed the book to the librarian.

"I see you found what you were looking for, I'm glad," the librarian said.

"Yes, this is the one I want."

While the librarian was checking it out, a well-dressed elderly gentleman with gray hair came in. He was about 5' 7", thin, dressed in a gray suit wearing a gray hat. The librarian quietly commented to Susan.

"He's one of the regulars that come in for the occult books. He never speaks or reads the book here, he goes to that section, gets a book, and checks it out. As I said before, weird, just weird."

Susan decided to wait at the counter to ask him a few questions. As he approached, she thought his face looked remarkably familiar, but from where."

"Excuse me, I've just become interested in reading about Stonehenge and the occult connected with it, could you give me any information on what I should read?"

Quickly replying, "Young lady, you're in a public library that has all you'll need to know about the subject," looking at his watch he continued, "I don't have time to speak to you now, but here's my card," pointing to the phone number printed at the bottom, "Call me at that number after 6 p.m."

"Thank you," she replied.

Placing his business card in the book, she left for home.

More than ever, the mystique of the strange scenes in the bottle intrigued her, and she wondered how far back in time the mysterious mist in the bottle would go. She thought, "I wish George was still alive so I could ask him questions. Could he have helped me? Was he able to see what I'm seeing in the mist? If he could, why didn't he mention it?" All these questions were turning over in her mind, as she left for home.

Chapter 6

Sitting at the dresser, Susan opened the book and began to read. From the limited understanding she had of the Druids, she always believed they were some sort of fanatic cult. Surprisingly, as she read, she discovered the Druids were a modern-day Professional Celtic Society, teachers, priests, philosophers, scientists and judges. Tapping her index finger on the bureau, she remembered the man that gave her the card in the library. His outward appearance didn't seem as though he would be interested in a radical cult. He looked more like a professional of some sort. She picked up the card he gave her to see if it had a business listing on it. No, it just had his name *Mr. Justin Stephens*, and a phone number.

Opening the parchment folder she began to read the strange words once again. *Shamhain, Shamhain, Shamhain.* Again the blue bottle became brighter. As she continued to read, the mist revisited the scenes of the dead Confederate soldier, then a Revolutionary War soldier. What could it mean?

The mist returned, and within a few minutes, cleared again, revealing a snowy scene of a hand carved village sign that read *York*. Arrows shot from bows were stuck in the sign, and a few on the sides of buildings. There were bodies of men and women lying on the ground dressed as Puritans. It appeared as though Indians had massacred villagers. A woman with a shawl over her head and shoulders came into the scene, and stood observing the aftermath of dead settlers. Susan could see she was holding a folder similar to the one she had. When the woman moved the scarf from her head and draped it over her shoulders, Sue quickly sat back. The woman's face was wrinkled, but she had long blond hair. Stopping for a moment, she thought,

"Why did the dresser go back to that scene? Was it to show her certain periods of time where the book was used? Did it have anything to do with where the dresser may have been at the time? What part did the blue bottle have at this period of history? "In thought, she gently ran her hand over the dresser's surface. She decided to return to the library and look up a town called *York*.

Putting on her coat, she returned to the library. Coming in the front door, the librarian looked up from her desk. "Back so soon?" she asked.

"Yes. I want to try looking up a town called *York*. It would have to be somewhere in New England."

The librarian replied, "What makes you think it was in New England? There are literally hundreds of towns bearing that name. Are you speaking past or present?"

"It would be past. There seemed to be a massacre of settlers in a small town. There was blood-stained snow on the ground, and by the looks of the clothes the dead were wearing, they appeared to be home spun. I believe it could possibly be early American, New England perhaps."

The librarian looked at Susan with great intent wondering, "How was she able to describe a scene so vividly?" Looking up the name York in the file cards, she discovered there was, a massacre in a town called York. It happened in what was then a Massachusetts colony. It took place on January 24th, 1692, where 100 English settlers were killed, and 187 people mostly women and children were captured.

Returning home, she began reading the words. As she read, the scene of the massacre returned. Again, she saw the old woman hold open the folder reading the words, and one of the dead men rose and followed her. Sue thought, "Why just a certain person? Was he related? Did these people in various periods of time have anything to do with a single event in the past? Was she a witch? If anyone saw her raise the dead, she would have certainly been tried for witchcraft. It was that period of time, between February 1692 and May of 1693? Yes, if anyone had seen her that would have surely been her fate.

What Susan was learning from the bottle's history was interesting, but it wasn't answering the one question she wanted to know. Why certain people were able to view the past, and others couldn't?

Turning her attention to the mist again, she could see what appeared to be a European castle. There were no significant features of the castle she could reference to, but she assumed it was somewhere between the 1400- 1500's.

All of a sudden the scene changed to a dungeon, where people were shackled to stone walls. The wails of the tortured, the moaning and lamenting of people reciting Christian sayings, were difficult to listen to. The scene showed robed people being herded into the dungeon like cattle, stripped and beaten. Could these be the worshipers of Stonehenge? Sue noticed amongst the people being shackled, an older woman with long, blond hair. Glancing up at the mirror, she thought, "I have long blond hair, would this, plus my ability in the psychic world, allow me to see what others can't?"

The mist in the bottle changed to what looked like those same hooded captives in a circle at Stonehenge holding hands. One of the members broke the chain entering the center of the circle, and the other members quickly closed ranks.

The central figure took a folder from her robe and began to read. *"Shamhain, Shamhain, Shamhain,* Oh god of earth and sky. Give us the sign of eternal life. Let not our enemies overpower your great ability." Then they all raised their arms toward the sky repeating, *"Shamhain, Shamhain, Shamhain."* The bottle seemed to focus on that period of time. Was it this group that gave the bottle its power?

Just then, the phone rang and the mist disappeared. Startled, she realized she was actually in a trance, somewhat like she experiences during a séance. Standing up, she gazed into the mirror. Surprisingly, she realized she was wearing the robe that was draped over the chair. She didn't recall putting it on. Looking down at it, she realized it was white, just as the members of the circle wore.

Diving across the bed to the phone on the end table, she answered it. "Hello!"

"Sue, this is Ray. Did I disturb you?"

"No, why do you ask?"

"I've called twice in the last half hour. I let the phone ring quite a long time before you answered. I was about to come over to see if you were ok."

Not wanting to share her trip back in time, she lied.

"I must have been in the shower. I'm fine."

"Did you call Delores to make the dinner arrangements?"

"No, no one's home, I'll call back in a half hour. Maybe she's out shopping."

After hanging up, I called Don at his office to ask him a question about the contract Mr. Johnson left for me to handle.

"Hello Don, this is Ray. I have a question for you."

"What is it Ray? I'm all ears."

"I have a contract here for a construction company. They list your company as a prior insurer. They're seeking a large liability policy, and I think they're having financial problems. I heard that from another source in the construction industry. Is there any way you can check it out for me?"

"Yes, I know somebody that can help. What's the name of the company?"

"They're listed as the Atlas Construction Company."

"You don't have to say anymore. That company changed its name three times in the last several years, they're a bad risk," Don said.

"Thanks, Don. I'll let Mr. Johnson know."

"Mr. Johnson. How is the old boy?" Don asked.

"He's doing fine. He just told me he's retiring in the spring. He said he can't take the cold any longer."

Don laughed, then asked, "Has Susan made any arrangements for dinner this week?"

"I just spoke to her. She said she tried to call Delores several times today, but she must not be home."

Don was silent for a few moments then replied, "That's funny. I just spoke to her and asked whether the new refrigerator has been delivered. She's been there all day. Is Sue sure she dialed the right number?"

Now I paused, "I don't know. At any rate, she wouldn't get it wrong several times. I wonder what's up. Maybe she just doesn't want to bother right now. She's been nursing a sore throat. In fact, she took off work today."

He went quiet on me again for a few moments, "That's funny. Delores said she had to run to the store for a few minutes, so she put a note on the door for the delivery men to wait until she returned. While she was leaving the store, she said she saw Sue coming out of the library. She called to her, but Sue either didn't hear her, or just wanted to get home. If she has a sore throat, she shouldn't be out in this weather. The wind with the flurries hitting your face, feels like a hand full of razor blades. I went out for lunch with a client."

"I know, I went out for a few minutes to grab lunch too. Thanks Don for the info on Atlas Construction. I really appreciate it."

"You're welcome. Let me know what Sue decides."

After hanging up, I realized subconsciously, I block lettered her name. Tapping the pencil on my desk, I thought about what Don said, "Why didn't she tell me she went to the library? Why did she tell me Delores wasn't home, when Don just told me she was there all day?" I picked up the phone deciding to call, but for some reason put it back down. Looking up at the clock, it was only 4:00. I still had another hour to go. I thought, "Maybe I should stop by her house unannounced on the way home?"

For the next hour, I kept busy dissecting the Atlas Policy, and with Mr. Johnson's approval, I composed a letter for our refusal to write it.

At 5:00, I straightened my desk and filed the copy of the letter, placing a red marker on the folder to identify it as a bad risk if they applied in the future. I put on my coat, quickly scanned the room then turned out the light. At the elevator, the waiting employees were abuzz with the snow falling. A man I knew from another office remarked, "I heard we're supposed to get 4 inches of snow tonight."

Another employee replied, "I heard that too. I hope the weather man's wrong. I live 25 miles from here. It's bad enough trying to get here with all the traffic when the weather's clear. It usually takes an hour. If the weatherman is right with his prediction, it will probably take 2 hours."

I thought about the 4 inches that was predicted, and wondered how many inches of snow Frank would get at the farm. The elevator doors opened, and I stepped aside allowing the ladies to get in first. Getting to street level, I could see a crowd of people standing by the front doors, gauging the best way to challenge the weather before exiting the building. My mind was on Susan, and I pushed through to the door and exited. Don was right, the wind drove the falling snow directly in my face, and I pulled my collar closed, lowering my head to keep it from getting in my eyes. I entered the parking garage, shook the lose snow from my coat, and stomped the snow off my feet before getting in my car. I started the engine, and rubbed my hands together waiting a few minutes until it began to warm.

Pulling out into traffic was a challenge, but a courteous driver stopped to wave me in front of him and I acknowledged his gesture with a wave. With the snow quickly piling up, I saw a few fender benders and decided to go straight home.

Before I took off my coat, I picked up the phone to call Sue, but didn't dial the number, wondering how to begin the conversation. Should I ask her what was so important at the library she had to risk getting sicker? If I do, she'll ask me how I knew she was there, then I'd have to tell her Delores saw her. I would then have to mention Delores being at home all day waiting for delivery men, and only running out for a few minutes. That in turn, would make her excuse for not being able to contact Delores to make dinner arrangements a lie. It would be painting her in a corner where she couldn't be seen as anything else. We didn't have any official attachments. We hadn't known each other that long, so I cradled the phone and looked at it a few moments. Did I do the right thing? I told myself I did, and took off my coat to prepare dinner.

For the most part, my preparation for dinner is popping one of those prepared TV dinners in the microwave. I had gotten used to them since my divorce two years ago. Now that I look back on it, they seem to taste better. I enjoy cooking if I have time, which is usually not the case. Opening the freezer, I went through the process of trying to decide. Should it be chicken, turkey, or roast beef tonight? Wait, there's lasagna. Since I obviously won't be enjoying that for dinner prepared by Sue, and probably won't be for the next two evenings, I might as well give it a try. I popped it in the micro and headed for the bedroom to change clothes.

Again, with the decision for dinner, I thought about Sue and why she was reluctant to make dinner plans. While I was sitting on the edge of my bed putting on my slippers I thought, "Why did she feel she had to lie? All she would have had to say is she didn't feel up to it."

Within a few minutes, the microwave alarm sounded dinner was ready. Using a pot holder, I lifted it out and peeled back the foil wrapping savoring the aroma. As I placed it on the table, I thought, "It isn't home made as I expected Susan's to be, but what the hell, I should be grateful I don't have to go out in this weather."

Passing by the kitchen window, I looked down at the lights of the parking lot swaying against the windblown snow, and watched as a few tenants ran from their cars to the front door of the building. I saw a tenant who lives several doors away, slip on the ice and fall. He recovered, and didn't appear to be hurt then hurried to the shelter of the lobby. I thought, "Maybe I should have gone to Susan's. Suppose she needs something. What good would I be to her if I'm a half mile away? Too late to think about that now, I'll call her later."

After dinner, I turned on the news wanting to catch the weather forecast for tomorrow. The person waiting for the elevator at the office said we were supposed to get 4 inches, but the weather man just revised the forecast to be between 4 and 6 inches. Well, I'm glad I'm home and made it without too much difficulty.

Just as I was getting comfortable, the phone rang.

"Hello. Who's calling?"

"Ray, this is Sue. I was just checking to make sure you made it home alright. I've been watching the news. They said with the ice under the snow, there are quite a few fender benders."

"I know Sue. I was looking out the window just now and saw a neighbor take a header on the parking lot coming to the building. He seemed to be alright. He got up and shook the snow off his clothes. I'm glad you're at home safe. I think it was the best thing for you to do with that sore throat."

"I'm feeling much better. Unless they call telling us our office will be closed for tomorrow, I'll have to brave the elements."

In the back of my mind, I wanted to ask her about not telling me the truth about calling Delores, but let it pass in favor of a more tactful approach.

I asked, "Did you happen to make any arrangements with Delores?"

"Yes, I just got off the phone with her. If it's ok with you, how about the day after tomorrow? Even if we get what they're predicting, it should be pretty much cleared away by then."

I replied, "Day after tomorrow it is. What can I bring, or how can I help you?"

"If you would stop at a liquor store to get a bottle of red wine that'll be helpful. You can also help with the hors d'oeuvres when you get here."

I jokingly remarked, "Madam, your wish is my command. Enough about me, what did you do today? I hope you relaxed as you promised."

She hesitated to answer for a few moments, then finally said, "I didn't budge from this bedroom."

A chill went up my spine. Why was she lying? What was she trying to conceal?

I was about to dispute her claim, when she quickly ended the conversation. I knew from several past experiences, she was able to read my mind and I thought, "Was this one of those occasions?"

"Ray, I think I better get something to eat. I haven't had anything since breakfast."

I replied, "Try some chicken soup, that's the cure all for colds and sickness."

She replied, "Maybe. That's what they say. George swore by it, and he reached the ripe old age of 95 or older."

"Goodnight Sue. I'll call you tomorrow."

I waited until she hung up before I hung up. If by chance she was reading my mind, I was hoping she knew it was only my concern for her, and not the control her former husband wanted. I tuned into a late evening TV program, and within 20 minutes, I was dozing off. Uncomfortable sleeping in a chair, I woke and turned off the TV and got ready for bed. I hadn't been in bed very long when the phone rang. Looking at my alarm clock, it was 12:30. I wondered, "Who could be calling me at this hour?"

"Hello!"

There was no answer, and I repeated myself, "Hello! Hello!" I demanded. In a quiet tone, Sue began to speak, "Ray, it's me. Sue."

"Why are you whispering?" I asked.

"I'm afraid to speak any louder, Someone's in the house."

I literally jumped out of bed reaching for my trousers. Trying to put them on while cradling the phone under my chin, I said, "Lock your bedroom door, right now!"

I was panic stricken. I could hear her movement following my command, and was desperately hoping I wouldn't hear a scream. After she returned to the phone, I felt relieved and asked, "Did you lock it?"

"Yes!"

"Do you still have a chair in the bedroom with you?"

"I have the bench seat that came with the dressing bureau. Why?"

"Try wedging it under the door knob, then call the police and give them your address. Do you have a gun in the house?"

"No, my ex took them with him."

"Don't panic. I'm getting my clothes on. I'll be there in 15 minutes."

"Wait! Don't hang up yet," in a horrifying quiet tone she begged, "Please hurry! I can hear a scratching at the bedroom door. Hurry! Hurry!

After hanging up, I immediately dialed the police explaining the situation and gave them her address. I told them there was an intruder in the house, and the resident locked herself in the bedroom and barred the door. I told them I was her boyfriend, and in route. The officer I was speaking to warned me of the hazardous driving conditions, but I paid little attention. After relaying my message, I called Sue again to tell her I too notified the police and was on my way.

The officer was right about the driving conditions, but since everyone heeded the weatherman's warning, the streets were relatively empty of traffic. As I approached each intersection where I was faced with a red signal, I slowed down and drifted forward, insuring there was nothing coming in a cross direction, then proceeded through the light. I had to slide to a halt several times before getting to Susan's street, and as I entered the block, I could see several flashing lights from police cars at her home. My heart was in my mouth wondering whether they were too late. Pulling up in the driveway, I was challenged by an officer standing outside his patrol car.

"Who are you?" he asked.

"Officer, I'm the one who called. This is my girlfriend's house. Is she ok?"

"Yes, a little shaken, but she's fine."

His words were a tonic that settled the uneasiness in my stomach. Going in the front door, I saw one of the officers standing in the living room with Susan. When she saw me, she threw her arms around my waist and put her head to my chest, breaking down crying. Patting her on the back, I said, "Officer, I'm Ray Bishop, Sue's boyfriend. Sue, are you alright?" I asked.

"Yes, I'm fine now that you're here. I was so afraid."

"Do you want me to put on a pot of coffee?"

"No, I'll do it," she replied.

When she went to the kitchen, I asked the officer, "Did you find anyone?"

He motioned for me to step into the hall leading to the bedroom. Following him I asked, "What is it officer?"

"I want to show you something," he replied. Pointing his flashlight at Susan's bedroom door, he asked, "Did you ever notice these marks before?"

I looked, and without any trouble, could distinctly see scratch marks on the painted surface. I replied, "They weren't here when we moved her dressing bureau here. They must be the marks from whoever was outside the door. On the phone, she did say she heard what sounded like someone scratching.

Do you know how, whoever it was, got in?"

His look of skepticism told me there was more to this than met the eye. I asked, "Officer, what are you trying to say?"

Looking at me, he quietly remarked, "I was the first officer at the scene. There were no footprints in the snow outside any of the windows around the house."

I asked, "Could it have possibly been her ex husband? I was told they had a bitter divorce."

"If it was her husband, he would have to have had the ability to levitate. The small snow drift at the front door was also undisturbed."

We went out to the living room as another officer entered the house asking, "Chief, should we resume patrol?"

"Yes, I'll only be a few more minutes." Turning to me in a quiet voice he asked, "Has Susan ever experienced hallucinations?"

Not wanting to disclose her psychic ability, I told him, "No." After seeing him to the front door, I thanked him and said goodnight.

Returning to the kitchen for the coffee, I asked, "Sue, are you sure you weren't dreaming, when you thought you heard someone in the house?"

She was pouring the coffee and turned to look at me seemingly annoyed at my accusation replying, "No. I couldn't have been dreaming. I heard someone walking in the hall and heard them scratching at the door."

I replied, "Well, there are scratches on the door, but are you sure they weren't there before, and possibly didn't notice them?"

Annoyed that I was questioning her, she replied, "No, they weren't there before. I watched closely when you and Don were carrying the dresser in, so you couldn't have done it."

Slowly looking up from my cup of coffee, I wanted to see her facial reaction to my next statement. I said, "The police didn't see any tracks in the snow anywhere around the house. Not even at the front door or garage door. If someone came in, they would have had to leave some kind of marks. It stopped snowing about an hour ago, so it's not likely they were there and covered up again," pausing, "I don't know what else to say."

She didn't answer, and I suggested, "Do you want me to stay the night? It's already 1:30? I could sleep on the sofa."

"You have to work in the morning. You won't be able to get a good night's rest that way. I'll be fine now that they checked the whole house."

"Ok, then, I'll leave after I finish this," lifting my cup as a gesture of acknowledgement. We talked about whether she should return to work in the morning. She decided she would, if the office was open.

After finishing the coffee, I put on my coat. She walked me to the front door, then embraced me, "Thanks for coming. I was so frightened."

Looking down at her face, I replied, "That's alright, I was frightened too. I almost got in an accident getting here as fast as I could."

She stood on her toes to give me a kiss on the lips.

I said, "Now that was worth the risk. Make sure you lock the door after I leave."

She smiled as I stepped out, and I could hear her throw the lock. Feeling confident she heeded my warning, I walked to my car. Driving home, I did it more cautiously.

I wondered why she was so adamant about her experience, when all the facts pointed to no one being there. If she was as good at being psychic, surely, she would know whether she was in danger. The whole thing was puzzling. When I got to my apartment, to be on the safe side, I called to make sure she was ok. She answered and said she was already tucked in bed. With that, I undressed and did the same.

***

Forgetting to set my alarm after coming home, I woke up late. It was already 5 minutes to 9:00. I called the office, and when my secretary answered, told me what I was hoping for didn't happen. I was hoping with the 6" of snow we got, the office would have been closed. I said to my secretary, "Mary, I'll be late this morning. I had to go out for an emergency at 1:00 a.m. If Mr. Johnson asks for me, tell him I'll explain it when I get there."

She sounded concerned and asked, "It wasn't a physical problem with you, was it?"

"No, nothing like that. Like I said, I'll tell you all about it when I get there." Looking at my watch I continued, "With these traffic reports I'm hearing. I'll probably get there around 10:30."

She replied, "I know. I left home a half hour early, and still got here just a few minutes before your call. If Mr. Johnson asks, I'll tell him."

"Thanks, Mary."

After hanging up, I dialed Sue's number. After she answered, I said, "Good morning. How did you sleep last night?"

Jokingly, she said, "I slept with one eye open, that's why I haven't left for work yet. I'm exhausted."

"You called off yesterday, why not call off again today?"

"No. This weather is a good excuse for being late."

"I know. I just called my office."

"You're still at home?" she surprisingly asked.

"Yes, I just wanted to check on you before I get showered and dressed. I'll call you around noon."

"Ok, that sounds good, and thanks again for last night."

I showered and quickly dressed, then left for work. Heading across the parking lot, I noticed the sky was clear but the wind was blowing strong. Dusty snow was blowing off the roof of the apartment building, and I hurriedly got in my car. Luckily, from clearing the snow off before going to Sue's, I didn't have to do it again. After the car warmed, I pulled out on the street and wove my way through traffic to the office parking lot. A parking spot in the company garage was one of the benefits of my job, and it came in handy on rainy or snowy days. After parking, I crossed the street and entered the building.

The first person I saw was Warren Simmons. He was engrossed in reading a contract as usual, and almost missed the open elevator doors. Looking down at his feet, I noticed he was still wearing his galoshes.

"Good morning Warren, did you make it to work on time?"

Looking up squinting over his thick glasses, he replied, "Yes, I left home at 6:00."

It brought a muted laughter from the elevator occupants, because most everyone knew he lived about a half mile from the building. Squinting again, he went right back to reading the contract. When the doors opened at the 4th floor, I exited. Mr. Johnson was leaving my office when he saw me.

Hurrying to meet me, he was holding the contract I advised him to reject.

"Ray, I read your note about this contract, is it true?"

"Yes, I'm afraid so Mr. Johnson. I found that out from a confidential source."

"Then I won't question it any further. Your secretary said you had an emergency of some sort during the night, is it something that's been taken care of?"

"Yes, the woman I've been dating had an intruder at 1:00 a.m. I wound up calling the police and rushing to her house to make sure she was alright."

"And I take it she was?" he replied.

"Yes, everything was handled by the police before I got there," not wanting to tell him it was a false alarm.

"That's good, that's good." he said as he walked away.

Entering the outer office, I related the same story to Mary- then went into my office closing the door behind me.

At 1 o'clock, I called Sue and asked, "What time did you finally get to work?"

"I wasn't that late. They decided to open an hour later."

"That's good, I'm glad. Are we still on for the dinner?"

"Yes. I told Delores to get to my place about 6. Dinner will be at 7. Is that ok with you?"

"Yes, and I won't forget the wine."

"That's good. I thought you may have forgotten with all the excitement. I'll see you at 5:30."

"I'll be there."

Chapter 7

I stopped at the liquor store on the way, and got the wine she wanted, and at 5:30 was knocking at her door. When she answered, I held up the bottle, "See, I didn't forget. Is this kind alright? It's a dry red wine. That should go well with lasagna."

Taking it from my hand, she examined the label and said, "I hope it isn't too dry. Dry wine gives me a headache."

"That's the best I could do, sorry."

"It will have to do. They'll be here in about a half hour. Come on, you can help me with the hors d'oeuvres."

The aroma from the lasagna made me realize how hungry I was. While she was standing at the sink, I put my arms around her giving her a hug, and kissing her lightly on the side of the neck, "The dinner smells delicious," I said, "What do you want me to do?"

"You can start by slicing the pepperoni and cheese. There's a serving tray in the top cabinet, don't slice the pepperoni too thick."

Taking the knife, I did as she asked, "Here, that's done. What else can I do?"

"You can set the table, and get the candle sticks from my bedroom. They're on the dressing bureau."

I thought it was strange she had them there. The last time I saw them, they were on each end of buffet. I wondered if she was tampering with a private séance. I shouted out from the bedroom, "I have the candlesticks but you'll need new candles. There's only about two inches left on these."

I noticed the book from the library about Druidism and opened the cover. I picked up the business card and read the name *Mr. Justin Stephens*.

I took the library card from the sleeve and looked at it. It was stamped with the date and time she was there. Why did she say she never left the house? Why did she lie? I quickly returned the card and closed the book.

I waited for a response to my question, and repeated myself, "Where are the new candles?"

After a few moments of silence, she entered the bedroom. Giving me a harsh look, she took the candlesticks from my hand, "I'll do it. Finish setting the table. They should be here soon."

The look on her face told me she was able to read my mind. Before I could say anything, she said, "I don't want you to question me about why I checked out this kind of book. It's something I've always been interested in."

I left the bedroom knowing for sure she was able to read my mind.

After placing the silverware and glasses on the table, the door bell rang. "I'll get it," I shouted.

Opening the door, a cold wind blew in. "Hi Delores, Don. Let me take your coats."

After Don helped Delores off with hers, he handed them to me, "Thanks, Ray. How did you make out with Atlas Construction?"

Delores quickly shut down our conversation, "No! No! No! No business talk tonight, we're here strictly for pleasure. Where's Sue?"

"She was in the bedroom looking for candles. She should be out momentarily."

Coming in from the bedroom, Sue embraced Delores and Don. "I'm glad we're finally getting together," Sue said.

Don remarked as he sniffed the aroma of the now finished casserole dish of lasagna on the counter. "No happier than I am. Sue, it smells good. Doesn't it Delores?"

Sue replied, "Well, have some hors d'oeuvres first."

Going to the dining room, she began searching the drawers of the buffet table, and china cabinet. "What are you looking for?" Delores asked.

Sue frustratingly replied, "I'm looking for the candles for the table. I'm not sure where I put them."

Delores replied, "Are you sure you didn't run out? We've had quite a few séances the last two months."

Sue replied, "I'm looking for the red tapors for the candlestick holders for the table." Opening the side door of the china closet she said, "I found them," then placed them in the holders on the table.

Making conversation, I said, "We had a little excitement here last night."

Delores quickly asked, "What kind of excitement?"

"Sue thought someone broke into the house. She locked the bedroom door and called the police."

Don, alarmingly asked, "Did someone break in?"

"No. It was a false alarm," I replied.

Delores said, "It wasn't a false alarm, it was real."

I replied, "No, I was here. There were no signs of anyone being around the house."

Don looked at Delores asking, "Why are you disputing Ray? He should know, if he was here."

"What are you talking about Don? I didn't say anything," she replied.

"Yes, you did. You said there was someone here, when Ray said there wasn't."

"I don't remember saying it," she replied.

Sue came from the kitchen. "I heard the conversation, how about letting it go for tonight and just enjoy dinner?"

I quickly remarked, "I think you're right."

After sitting at the table, we raised our wine glasses to toast the evening.

Don asked, "Who was the gentleman coming from the house when we pulled into the driveway?"

"What gentleman Don?" I asked, "We've been here by ourselves since 5:30."

Giving me a strange look, he replied, "There was an elderly gentleman coming down the walk. Maybe he realized he was at the wrong house and never knocked."

Sue was lifting her glass to her mouth then suddenly put it down, "What did he look like?" she asked, with a concerned look.

Delores answered, "He was an elderly gentleman, very distinguished looking."

Sue stopped for a moment staring at her glass. I didn't have to be a psychic to realize she was very concerned at what the answer might be to her next question. "Delores, how was he dressed?"

Don replied instead, "He was wearing a long gray overcoat with a gray dress hat. I couldn't see it all, but he looked like he was wearing a suit coat and tie."

Listening to Don's description, I looked over at Sue, and noticed her hand begin to shake. I asked, "Sue, what's wrong? Are you alright?"

"Yes, I'm fine," she replied.

Delores surprised Sue with her next comment, "Sue, could it be the man I saw coming out of the library just before you left it the other day? I watched as he stood in the doorway of a clothing store further down the block. I thought he was just looking at the merchandise in the window, but after you walked by, he seemed to be interested in where you were going. The strange part about it, the man that was leaving here was dressed the same, identically."

Sue was surprised, and her face became flush with embarrassment. I think she was more embarrassed that she was exposed as telling me a lie, than her immediate concern for the stranger. She replied to Delores, "I didn't know you saw me at the library. Why didn't you say something?"

"I did, but I don't think you heard me. Besides, I was home all day waiting for delivery men to bring the new refrigerator, and didn't want to stay away too long."

Looking down at her wine glass during Delores' remarks, she suddenly looked at me. "Ok Ray, I lied to you that I didn't go out the other day. I didn't want you to be mad at me for going out when I was sick. That's all it was."

"Sue, you don't have to defend yourself from me. I just don't know the reason you think you have to."

Delores remarked, then smiled while she lifted her glass, "Can we change the conversation and talk about the weather or something?"

Don replied, "We can talk about this delicious meal."

"Yes, it sure is Don," I replied.

As hard as it was trying to force conversation to salvage the evening, there was an uneasy feeling in the room for the rest of the night. It was so prevalent- Delores and Don decided to leave shortly after dessert. I thought, "Did I bring this uneasy feeling on, or was it Sue, feeling she had to justify her actions? Did Delores stir up something, when she described the man that left the library, looking like the same man that was coming from the house?" Something didn't seem quite right.

After bidding Delores and Don goodnight, I asked, "Sue, you seemed to be withdrawn after Delores mentioned the library. I assure you, I didn't think anything of it, I was only concerned for your well being," adding a joke trying to sooth the tension, "After all, I can't have you quit on me now. We have a lot of work to do at the farm in the spring."

It seemed to break the tension, and I poured another glass of wine. Thinking we could relax sitting on the sofa for awhile, I asked, "Do you want to join me?"

I was surprised at her reply, "I don't think so. I already have a headache from drinking the wine at dinner. Remember, I told you dry wine does that to me."

"That's right! Can I get you an aspirin or something?"

"No, I think I'll just go to bed early tonight. If you'll excuse me, it's been a long day."

Her words were a shock to me, and I realized the excuse about having a headache was only to get me to leave. I rose from the sofa, put the wine glass on the kitchen counter, and headed for my coat in the closet. Seeing I felt a little dejected, she came to me and put her arms around my waist. She looked up at my face, and shook her head, stammering for the right words to apologize.

"I'm, I'm sorry Ray. I'm just not myself today. I can't imagine I'm treating you like this; after all you did for me last night. I'm really sorry."

Passing off her comment, I replied, "Don't worry. Take care of that headache," then kissed her forehead saying, "Goodnight Sue."

Driving home, for some reason, I began to feel uneasy. I remembered

Delores commenting after the séance at the farm. 'People that are being possessed don't realize it, but the people that are associated with them, will definitely notice the difference.'

I repeated it in my mind, again and again, as I drove home. Why did she check out a book from the library on Druidism? Why were the candlesticks on the dressing bureau? If the blue bottle wasn't there, what was filling the space between the candlesticks? Suddenly, I pulled to the curb thinking, "Should I go back? No, what excuse would I have without knowing for sure whether there was a problem? I'll go home and call Delores. Maybe she'll have an answer."

Before I could dial Delores's number, the phone rang. I expected it to be Susan apologizing again, but it wasn't.

"Hello. Who's calling?"

"Ray, this is Delores. What's wrong between you and Sue? I've never known her to act that way. What happened the other night when she called the police?

Is it some___," Before she could finish battering me with all the questions, I shut her down.

"Whoa! Whoa! Slow down. Give me a chance to speak and I'll tell you. She called me the other night at 1:00 a.m. and told me she heard someone walking around in the house. I instructed her to lock her bedroom door and bar the handle with a chair, then asked if she called the police? She said she had, and I told her I would be there as fast as I could. She told me to hurry, there was someone scratching at her bedroom door. I asked if she had a gun in the house, and she said she didn't. I asked if she was sure she gave the police the right address, and she said she had. She spoke hurriedly, but had all the answers, so I know she wasn't just waking up from a bad dream. She seemed to have her faculties in order. After I hung up, I called the police too, just to make sure."

"What happened then?" Delores asked.

"I got dressed as fast as I could, and drove to her house. When I arrived, the police were already there. They checked all the windows and doors, but didn't find anything. The one officer I spoke to pointed out that the deep snow around the house was undisturbed."

"How about the front door?" she asked, "Sue did go through a hell of a battle with her ex. Maybe it was him?"

"I spoke to the sergeant at the scene, and asked if the intruder could have gone in through the front door, thinking it may have been her ex too. I already knew they had a bitter battle. Don told me. The sergeant said he was the first person at the scene, and reassured me by saying, 'Even the snow outside the front door was undisturbed.'

He suggested it may have been a bad dream, and I think Susan was pissed he implied that. Without physical evidence of an entry, he couldn't be disputed."

"Did you see anything unusual?" Delores asked.

"I looked outside of her bedroom door and there were some scratch marks. I made the suggestion, that Don and I could have accidently done that moving in the dresser, or maybe she just never noticed them. That's when she really looked annoyed at me. It was as though she thought I was looking for an excuse not to believe her."

"Did you stay the night?"

"No, she seemed to want me to leave, so I did. Before I left though, she did apologize. The man you said you saw tonight that you thought was leaving the house, are you sure he was the same man that followed her from the library?"

"I'm almost positive."

I remarked, "Tonight when Sue told me to get the candlesticks from the bedroom, I noticed a book on her dressing bureau. It was about Druidism. When I opened the book, I found a card, you know, like a business card. It only had a name and phone number on it."

Delores replied, "Maybe someone that had the book before used the card as a marker, and forgot to take it out. What was the name?"

"If I can remember right, the name sounded very distinguished. Wait a minute, let me think. I remember now, it was Justin Stephens. Does it ring a bell from any of your psychic encounters?"

"I'll have to check. I keep notes of the different readings I give. Maybe something will show up there."

"Anything you can do to help, I'd appreciate. I really don't want to lose this relationship."

After my conversation with Delores, I took out a few insurance policies I wanted to work on, but before I was finished the first one, the phone rang.

"Hello, who's calling?"

"It's me, Susan. If it's not too late, can you come over?"

I was surprised. She didn't seem panicky and I hesitated to answer for a few moments, wondering whether I heard her right.

"What's wrong?" I asked.

"There's nothing wrong, I just didn't want to be alone tonight. I have a bad feeling. I don't know why, it's something I can't put a finger on."

"I'll bring my clothes and leave for work from there."

"Thanks Ray. Try to hurry."

Quickly gathering a shirt, pants, and underclothes, I put them in a long clothing bag along with my toothbrush, underarm deodorant, and shaving gear in the side pocket, then left.

Pulling into the street, I could see a man standing on the sidewalk looking at Susan's house. I slowed down to get a better look, and noticed from the glow of the streetlight, he was an older man, dressed in a long gray overcoat with a gray hat. The same description of the man Delores and Don saw, when they were coming to dinner. I came to a near stop and rolled down my window.

"Hey what are you doing?" I shouted.

Seeing me, he quickly turned, walking away.

I called out again, "Who are you? What do you want?"

He ignored my remark, and continued walking, looking back over his shoulder, to insure I wasn't following. I became panic stricken. Had he been in Susan's already? I threw the car into drive and turned into her driveway. Exiting the car, I was relieved when her porch light went on. That meant she was safe, and was waiting for me to arrive.

Stamping the snow from my feet before entering, I closed the door.

Excitedly I asked, "Sue, what makes you have this bad feeling? Is it a premonition of something that's going to happen?"

Drawing close, she put her arms around my waist. Looking around the room as if there was someone within hearing distance, she quietly said. "I don't know. I never experienced this before. It's like someone's watching me. I can't explain it any better than that."

I was going to ask about the man looking at the house, but thought, It might only heighten her fear, so I didn't mention it.

"Would you like some coffee?" she asked.

Looking at my watch, I replied, "Don't you think it may be a little late? It might keep you awake."

"I have decaf, that shouldn't bother me."

"Ok, then I'll have a cup."

Sitting at the kitchen table, I asked, "Sue, when you were at the library, did you see a well dressed elderly man in a suit with a long gray overcoat and hat?"

Suddenly looking up, she replied, "Yes, why?"

"Delores said she saw a man dressed like that follow you after you left the library."

"That's impossible. He left before me."

"Well, Delores saw him waiting outside a store and after you left, he seemed to be following you. She said she seen what looked like the same man coming from your house."

"When was that?"

"The night they came to dinner. They thought he was here but he couldn't have been. I was here, remember?"

"That's right, so how could he have been here?"

"He couldn't. I don't want to alarm you, but there was a man standing on the sidewalk just now, looking at the house when I pulled up. He was dressed the same way Delores described. When I called to him, he hurriedly walked away."

"Well that does upset me. Maybe I can exorcize the blue bottle to give me an answer."

Following her to the bedroom, I watched as she carefully took the bottle from the dresser drawer. Picking up the book on Druidism, I examined the cover and asked, "What's the book on Druidism for?"

Quickly taking it from my hand, she said, "I picked it up from the library to check something out. I wondered if this blue bottle has any connection with them."

My enthusiasm built, "Why do you think that? Do you think George's grandmother practiced that religion?"

"I don't know, but I intend to find the mystery behind this bottle, and why only I can see the mist in it."

Quickly replying, "No one else sees it but you. How do you account for that?"

Ignoring my question, we went back to the kitchen table. She opened a drawer retrieving two pieces of paper with the word *YES* and *NO* written on them. By having them, it was obvious she wanted to have a séance long before now, but for some reason didn't want to ask.

"Here, sit opposite me," she asked, "There's only the two of us, so you'll have to ask the questions."

"I thought there had to be at least four people?"

"Generally, you do, but we don't have four, so we'll try it with just the two of us."

"Ok, what shall I ask?"

"Start by asking if there's a purpose with me being the only person that's able to see the mist. If it points to the word *Yes,* ask what that purpose is. If it gives you a *No,* clap your hands loud to end the séance."

"Suppose it says *Yes*- what shall I ask then?"

"Ask if it's something about the bottles past. If it says *Yes,* ask what period of time? You might be able to go back by years. For example; ask if it's 50 years. If it points to *No,* ask if it's 80 years, and so on, until you get a *Yes.* After you get the right period of time, ask whether it has anything to do with George or his great grandmother."

Looking skeptical, I replied, "Ok, I'll give it a try. Where are the candlesticks?"

Mist in the Blue Bottle

"They're in the spare bedroom on the shelf."

Coming back to the kitchen, I lit the candles and turned out the lights. Sue bowed her head as she had in the séances at the farm, and after a few moments, her hair fluffed up. I knew from seeing it before, she was ready.

I asked, "Is there anyone present that can give us the answers about the mist in the bottle?"

The bottle slowly turned to the word *Yes*.

"Is this person George?" to my surprise, the bottle slowly turned to the word *No*."

"Who am I in the presence of?"

Sue slowly lifted her head, peering straight into the darkened room, and began to speak words that didn't seem to make sense. "Samhain, Samhain, Samhain. Arawn, Cernunnos, Cerriowen, Rhiannon, Taranis- Goddeses- and Gods, I am all."

Although the words were strange and incoherent, Susan didn't appear to be in any danger so I continued.

"Are you the spirit of George Berkley's great grandmother?"

The bottle gently spun pointing to the word *Yes*. I asked, "Is George there with you?"

The bottle turned two revolutions and stopped, surprisingly, pointing to the word *No*. I was expecting the opposite answer then continued, "Why isn't he there with you?"

Sue answered in a gentle voice, "He doesn't have the power."

All of a sudden something came to mind. I remembered George telling Sue when he gave her the bottle, 'My great grandmother and grandmother had the power, but I didn't have it to talk in the spirit world.' Maybe that's what he was trying to tell us? Maybe that's the power he was trying to explain?

I asked, "Does Susan, the person you're speaking through have the power?"

The bottle turned abruptly to the word *Yes* then turned itself upright. A strange mist appeared in the bottle, and for the first time I could see it. The voice within Susan spoke, "Yes, she's the chosen one."

I asked, "What does she have to do?"

In a commanding voice from the spirit within Susan, replied, "Obey the Gods."

"How will she know what to do?"

"It's been passed down through the centuries. When she comes, she will know."

Annoyed at the idea Sue might be taken against her will, I quickly blew out the candles. For a brief moment before turning on the lights, I looked toward the closed living room drapes. I could see a shadow of a man appearing to be looking in the living room illuminated by the street lights behind him. Without putting on the lights, I went to the window and quickly pulled the strings opening the drapes. The shadow was gone. Leaving Sue in her transcendental state, I slipped on my coat and opened the front door. I looked at the snow in front of the picture window where I saw the shadow, but the snow was undisturbed. I thought, "Was I hallucinating? I couldn't be; it was real." It looked like the same figure of the old man I saw standing in front of the house.

Going back inside, I clapped my hands loud as Sue directed me, and she came out of her trance.

"What happened?"

"Look, Sue, don't you think it's getting late for this discussion? I think we should discuss it tomorrow."

"Ok, but promise me it's only because of the lateness of the hour."

"That's what it is. If I start, we'll be up all night. I'm really tired. Where do you want me to sleep?" jokingly continuing, "With you I hope."

She smiled replying, "Then you'll never get any sleep. I wouldn't want you to miss your beauty rest."

"I got the message," looking down at the sofa, "I guess this is my bunk for tonight?" I said.

"That's it. I'll get you a pillow and blanket."

In a few minutes she returned and we kissed goodnight. After brushing, I slipped under the blanket and turned out the lamp. Instinctively, I looked toward the closed drapes, but to my relief, the shadow wasn't there. To my joy, whoever it was didn't return, and I was happy to be able to close my eyes and sleep.

***

I awoke in the morning to the smell of coffee being brewed. Sitting up, I said in a loud tone, "Smells good!"

Thinking Sue was in the kitchen, I peeked in, but she wasn't there. I could hear the water running in the shower, so I poured a cup for myself, and returned to the living room. I put on the TV to listen to the weather report, and disappointedly, they predicted more snow for the weekend. In a few minutes, Sue entered the room. I looked, and then smiled with a slight chuckle.

"What's so funny?" she asked.

"Standing there in your robe with the towel wrapped around your wet hair, you look like a swami. You know, fortune teller. It sure fits with what took place last night."

She replied, "Remember the day we met when we were going to the farm for the first time? You promised you wouldn't make fun of the psychic world."

"Yes, I remember. I'm sorry, I was only kidding."

"I assumed that, but remember, you said you were going to tell me everything that happened last night."

Picking up my watch from the end table, I looked at the time. "Damn, it's almost 7:30. I better get showered and dressed, I have an early appointment."

"Well, pick me up after work and we can go out to dinner. You can tell me then."

Without telling her about the shadow on the drapes, I asked, "Who is *Justin Stephens?*"

She suddenly turned serious and looked at me, "How do you know that name?"

"His card was in that book on your dresser. Who is he?"

She hesitated, but couldn't deny her knowledge, "I met him in the library. He's very versed on the Druid society. I thought I could call on him if I had any questions."

She tried to mask her interest by saying, "Why? Are you jealous?"

"No, I just thought I'd ask. I better head for the shower; it's getting late."

Before closing the bathroom door she asked, "How about a light breakfast, toast, or an English muffin?"

Before closing the door I replied, "English muffin will be fine."

Letting the warm water run down my body, I thought about how my conversation about the private séance should go, "Should I invite Delores? Or would Sue be offended and think it was only supposed to be between her and I?" Enough thought. I had to get dressed and get to work.

Quickly dressing, I headed for the kitchen. After a few bites of English muffin and a few gulps of coffee, I was ready to face the day. I headed for the car as Susan was locking the front door. Getting in the passenger side she snuggled close until the car warmed.

I said, "That's the closest you've been to me all morning."

She looked up at me with a smile, after kissing her finger tips she placed them on my lips. I returned the smile saying, "I'll pick you up at 5:30, how's that?"

"That will be fine. It's Friday and the restaurants will be crowded. I'll make reservations this afternoon. Where would you like to dine?" she asked.

"Any place you want will be fine with me. Make sure it's someplace we can talk."

Hesitating for a moment, giving it some thought, she replied, "Maybe we should go to my house or your apartment?"

I really didn't want to go back to her house, and thought a change of environment would be better to discuss what happened. Instead of being objective, I was getting caught up with my own emotions.

"We'll make it my apartment. We can always order a pizza or something quick." I hesitated before asking, "Should I invite Delores and Don? We can have a regular party."

"If you don't mind, I'd like to do this by ourselves."

The ride to work was quiet, and I wondered whether it was because she was reading my thoughts. Pulling up in front of her building, I caught site of something that sent a shock through my body, and I could feel the hair on the back of my neck raise. Standing in a doorway of a store that hadn't yet opened for business, was the same elderly man I seen the night before, outside Susan's house.

I thought, "Is he a stalker?"

I knew Susan didn't see him when she opened the car door, and I said goodbye as she walked toward her building. I wanted to park to see what he would do as she entered the building, but the traffic behind me was impatient, quickly letting me know by blowing their horns. It attracted the old man's attention, and he looked in my direction. I believe he recognized my car because he stepped from the doorway and briskly began walking down the street, opposite my direction. I was able to manage getting around the block quick enough to catch a glimpse of him, looking back to where he thought I might be trying to park. I pulled over and exited the car as he approached the corner. He didn't see me until he turned, and I blocked his path. Taking a hold of his sleeve, I spun him around and pulled him to the side. It startled him, and he was obviously surprised at being so violently confronted.

"Who are you? What do you want with Susan? Why are you following her?" I demanded.

Flustered by the confrontation, he took a few moments to respond to my hostility and the barrage of questions. Unsure of my actions, he nervously replied, "I__ I don't mean to do her any harm. We met in the library earlier this week. She asked me for information about Druidism. I gave her my card."

"Then you're Justin Stephens!" I replied.

"That's right. I'm a professor of Ancient English History."

I eased my grip on his sleeve, and let him know in no uncertain terms, I didn't like his intrusion in her life without asking. He replied with a strange look on his face, "She did ask. She called me the same night I gave her my card. Didn't she tell you? We even had a meeting with my fellow members."

I couldn't dispute what I didn't know, and let go of his arm.

"I'm sorry. She never told me, I didn't know." Not wanting to hurl another accusation without first speaking with Susan, I said, "If you'll excuse me, I have to get to work."

He replied, "I know, you work for Keystone Insurance Company. Your name is Ray Bishop. How would I know that unless she told me?"

He was right, I was beginning to see there was more to this than Sue was telling me. Returning to my car, I watched as Justin quickly retreated into the crowd of pedestrians, looking back several times to make sure I wasn't following.

On the way to the office, I was tossing around in my mind what he said about the meeting. Where could it have been? It couldn't have been at Susan's. The snow outside the house was undisturbed as the officer said. That thought really shook me up. Did the blue bottle have the ability to transport people through time? It did have the power to come back to its original form after being smashed against the wall at the séance with George- I wonder?

Chapter 8

I was busy in the office for the first few hours, and I found it hard to concentrate on my work. Around 11:00, there was a knock at the door. Before I could say come in, Mr. Johnson entered the room with a contract in his hand. He was obviously annoyed, and I automatically assumed it was a screw up on my part. He said in an upsetting tone, "Ray, this contract you put together, it leaves the company at too much risk. Why didn't you consult me first?"

He was right. I had no defense. I've been neglectful with my work dealing with Sue and her situation. I replied, "I'm sorry Mr. Johnson. I guess I thought I had everything covered to protect the company. The premium is higher so I thought with the company's past record, it wouldn't be a bad risk."

It seemed to settle him a little, but I could tell he still wasn't comfortable with my answer. It was one of those times where I took a chance on throwing the dice, hoping a 7 wouldn't appear.

"I hope you're right Ray, but the next time, consult me first."

"I will Mr. Johnson, I apologize."

After he left my office, I stood next to the window with my arms folded looking out, thinking about what just transpired. The last person on this earth I wanted to disappoint was Mr. Johnson. He had so much confidence in me, that this small confrontation made me feel unworthy to take the reins after his retirement.

Suddenly I noticed something across the street. The old man I confronted this morning was standing in the doorway with an older woman. He pointed up at my window and for some reason, I stepped back trying to hide from their view. I thought, "Why did I do that? Why are they following me?"

My attention quickly returned to having a better interest in doing my job and knuckled down to correct it.

Around 2:00 I phoned Delores. I first made her promise that my confidence in her silence wouldn't be misplaced, then began filling her in on what's been happening. She listened intently, knowing from my concern with Susan I wouldn't be telling a lie. After telling her about the confrontation I had with Justin, I told her about the meeting he mentioned with a few of his friends and Sue. Delores went silent on me for a few moments, then asked, "Did Justin say where the meeting took place?"

"No, I didn't think about asking. Is it important?"

For the second time she went silent, and I had to repeat myself to get a response. I knew she was hesitating on purpose and wondered why?

"Ray, I don't want to upset you, but I think you're in deeper than you suspect. She's becoming a cult member."

"You mean like a group thing, where they sit around and have séances to bring back the dead?"

"In a way, yes, she may be taking on a spirit of someone in the bottle's past history. What can you tell me about the séance last night?"

"We used the blue bottle just like we used it at the farm. There was only the two of us, and I asked if we needed four. I remembered that's what you said the first time you were at the farm. Remember? Frank and June didn't want to do it, that's when we got George."

"I remember. But you do need four to complete the circle. Two can't do it unless there were two other people present. Did you sense anyone else there?"

"Come to think about it, I asked whether George's great grandmother, or grandmother was present. The bottle pointed to the word *YES,* and said it was George's grandmother. I asked if George was there, and it pointed to the word *NO.* When I asked why, Sue replied he didn't have the power. Remember George told us that?"

"Yes, I do. If I were you, I'd be a little cautious about being in her company."

I replied in a frustrating tone, "What do you mean? I've fallen in love with her."

"Yes, I know, but you have to remember, it isn't her that's there. She's being controlled by someone that might not like your attachment. When are you supposed to see her again?"

"We're going to my apartment after work. She made me promise to tell her what happened last night while she was in a trance. It was too late to get into a conversation last night, and we didn't have time to get into it this morning. I did see the man you said you saw coming from her house when you and Don came for dinner. It was Justin. Whatever attachment or meeting he has with Sue, must have taken place in her home."

"What makes you think that?"

I replied, "Before the séance last night, I saw his shadow behind the drapes. It looked like he was looking in at me, but the drapes were closed. When I went outside to see what he wanted, he wasn't there, he had disappeared. What really upset me, I noticed there weren't any tracks in the snow where he was standing. It was weird. Why did he think he could see us through the closed drapes?"

Another moment of silence, then she replied, "No, he was there looking at you. Remember, he's only a manifestation of someone."

"But he couldn't be. He was outside Susan's building this morning, watching as she got out of my car. He walked away, but I was able to catch up to him at the corner. I grabbed him by the arm. I swear he was real."

"No, he only appeared to be real. Sometimes they can manifest themselves into any physical form they want."

"Now you're really scaring me. What am I going to do about someone that isn't real?"

"You're supposed to go to your apartment tonight- right?"

"Yes, right after work. Why?"

"I was thinking that Don and I could just accidently on purpose stop by. Maybe we can join in on the discussion."

"I hate to bring it up, but I suggested that you get involved this morning. When I did, she became angry, and made it known your being included was unwanted. You're great friends, why would she say that?"

"Remember, she isn't the person you're speaking to some of the time."

"You mean like a dual personality?"

"No, you're dealing with two different people. When we get there, just mention last night mildly. I can take it from there."

I replied, "We'll be at my apartment around 6:00. Thanks Delores."

After work I swung by and picked up Susan. Surprisingly she asked, "Why did you confront Justin this morning?"

"How did you know I did? You went in the building. I didn't think I saw him."

"I didn't. We met at the cafeteria. He bought my lunch. I never knew it until today, but he's a big stock holder in our bank."

I defensively fired back, "Well, why didn't you tell me before that you knew him?"

Adamantly, she replied, "I didn't know him. Those depositors are reserved for the upper echelon in the bank, Vice President or President. That's how important he is. I only deal with the lower depositors- from $500,000 to 1 million. Believe it or not, the people with the lesser amount, are a bigger pain in the ass than the biggest depositors."

I replied, "It's probably because they already have as much as they want. What else could it be?"

"That's pretty perceptive, and pretty much the truth too."

I pried a little more, "If you don't deal with his account, how did you happen to go to lunch with him?"

I heard a siren coming at a cross intersection, and stopped to let it pass. It was a perfect opportunity for her to have time enough to gather a response.

"He saw me walking through the lobby and stopped to say hello. It was close to 12:00 and he asked me if I was going to lunch. I told him yes, and he asked if he could go with me. That's all."

Not wanting to sound like a control freak, I asked, "If you don't mind me being nosey, what did you talk about?"

"We discussed the Druids. He knows a lot about the religion. He got his doctorate on the subject of Ancient English History."

She began to rattle on about their conversation, and it was obvious his hold on her was more than just an interest on the subject. Was he targeting her spirit for inclusion into his society? Remembering what Delores said about a spirit manifesting itself to be almost real, I asked, "What did you have for lunch?"

"I had a grilled cheese sandwich with tomato and__" Before she was finished her menu I interrupted__ "And what did Justin have?"

She looked angrily at me, realizing my question toward her, was only to get answers about Justin. With an angry tone in her voice she demanded, "Why are you asking what he had?"

"Just curious, that's all."

She seemed to accept my answer, and it appeared to smooth the tension between us, but I still had the feeling she didn't believe me. That's one of the things I didn't like about being in her company, she was able to read my thoughts.

After pulling into my apartment parking lot, we entered the building. Seeing Don and Delores in the lobby, I acted surprised, "Hi guys. What are you two doing here?"

Don replied, "We were just passing on our way out to dinner, and thought you might like to join us?"

I realized Delores must have prompted Don to initiate the conversation to let Sue think the timing was coincidental. I played along and was hoping Sue with her ability wouldn't see through the ruse.

Don continued, "I didn't know you were here Sue," then embraced her. Sue embraced her in kind, but I could tell the gesture was half hearted.

I said, "We were going to order pizza and discuss a private séa__. I didn't get séance out, but only enough to arouse Delores's response. She said, "Were you going to say private séance? When did this take place?" she excitedly asked.

I looked at Sue. She seemed to be angry at my blunder, but didn't comment. I replied, "Sue and I had a private séance last night. Come on up and we'll tell you all about it. First I want to order the pizza. Don, I know you like anything on your pizza. Delores, I know you like pepperoni.

Sue we never had pizza together, so I don't know what you prefer. What would you like?"

"I like mine plain."

After ordering, I poured drinks for everyone and we sat down in the living room. Delores was the first to open the conversation, "Sue, who else was at the séance beside you and Ray?"

She knew Delores was aware that you had to have four people, but didn't respond. I looked at Sue then played dumb by saying, "It was only the two of us."

Delores played the part well, acting surprised. Looking at Sue she asked, "Just the two of you! How can that be Sue?"

Sue replied, "I wasn't sure whether it would work, but it did. Ray asked the questions and the blue bottle gave the answers. I don't know what I said. It was too late last night to get into it, and not enough time this morning. That's why we came here. We were going to discuss what happened."

Delores replied, "Well I'm glad we stopped. Ray, tell us what you asked."

"I wasn't sure what to ask. Sue gave me instructions to try and find out what period of time we were dealing with."

"Dealing with what?" Delores asked, first looking at me, then at Sue.

Interested myself, I looked at Sue to begin telling Delores what the séance was for. Looking away from me, she said, "I've been trying to figure out the power of the blue bottle. I was focused on it the day after I brought it back, and the same mist appeared as I saw at George's. It suddenly cleared and I wondered what was causing it, that's all."

She only mentioned the mist. It was obvious she didn't want to divulge too much. Her statement warranted more of an answer, and I knew Delores must have realized it. I couldn't take it any longer and jumped up from my chair. Slapping my hand on the table, I shouted, "God damn it Sue! Tell her what the hell happened. If you don't, I will."

I surprised Sue with my hostile reaction, and she chose to remain silent. I took it upon myself to expose more of what took place, relating the events of the evening. After exposing what took place, Delores sat dumfounded for a few moments before asking, "Sue, why didn't you tell me this? We've been friends for a long time."

I looked at Don and realized he was getting uncomfortable with the conversation, but remained silent.

Delores looked at Sue then asked, "What else did you have Ray ask the bottle?" becoming indignant that Sue excluded her from the séance.

Sue seemed to take on her normal mood again and embarrassingly replied, "I'm sorry Delores. I really didn't want to bother you. I thought I could figure it out myself."

I quickly added, "Delores, I asked if it was George's great grandmother or grandmother. The bottle gave me the answer that it was his grandmother."

Don joined the conversation, "Did you ask if George was with her?"

"Yes. She said he wasn't. He didn't have the power. Do you remember him telling us that Delores?"

She replied, "Yes, maybe that's what he meant when he told us that. What else did you discover?"

"Before Sue went into her trance she asked me to try and find out the age of the bottle by going back in 100 year increments. The bottle kept giving me a *NO* until I hit upon the 15 century.

That's when I saw the shadow of a man outside the closed drapes."

Delores quickly interrupted, "What man! Who was it?"

Replying, "I don't know but he interrupted my chain of thought. When I went outside to see who it was, there was no one there."

Delores looked at Sue then asked, "Well Sue, who was outside?"

"I don't know. I have a feeling whoever it was, wants me to discover the origin of the bottle, for whatever reason. That's why I had only Ray do the séance with me. I'm trying to find out the bottles age by going back in time increments. Maybe it wants me to understand the origin of its power."

"And did you?"

Delores looked at me and before I could answer, Sue quickly said no."

Delores asked looking at Sue, "No! No what Sue?"

"I didn't say anything," she replied.

"Yes you did. You answered no."

"I don't remember saying it."

Don said, "Can we lay this conversation aside for awhile, it's giving me the creeps."

"You're right Don," I replied.

Just then the doorbell rang. Realizing it must be our pizza delivery person, I got up to answer it. After taking the boxes, I paid him and he promptly left.

Don opened the first box, and the aroma from the piping hot delight, made me realize I was hungrier than I thought. Maybe it was the conversation? I didn't know, but I realized Delores and my conversation was far from over, it would continue.

During our meal Delores asked, "Ray did you ever find out how far back the power of the bottle went?"

Sue suddenly seemed to want to add to the conversation. "I saw several visions from the bottle's mist. One was the scene of the Confederate soldier, and another of a Revolutionary War soldier. They were sitting in a rocking chair on the porch of a log cabin, but they were both dead."

"How do you know they were dead?" I asked.

"I could see blood on their shirts. It was probably from a bullet wound."

Don asked, "Were they in the same time period?"

"No, it was separate, but the old woman was the same person, I know it."

Don put down his slice of pizza and replied, "Then it must have been from separate wars. They were over 80 years apart."

"Yes, I know, but the woman was the same person. That's what I couldn't understand."

Delores asked, "You say the woman had long blond hair. It didn't change with age?"

"No, she was the same, an old woman with a wrinkled face. She was sitting next to them reading from an old leather bound folder."

Delores asked, "What was she reading?"

"I don't know. They were strange words I couldn't understand. After she finished reading, she closed the folder and went into the cabin. In a few minutes the soldiers opened their eyes and followed her."

"Then you're saying she had the power to bring back the dead?"

"That's the only way I can see it, but why only show me. Delores, you looked at the bottle and saw a mist but no scenes. Ray looked at it and couldn't even see the mist. I think having some psychic ability allows us to see it Delores, but in different degrees. My ability seems to exceed yours."

Don mesmerized by the conversation, was still holding his slice of pizza. The pointed end was drooping and there was no steam coming from the slice, it had gotten cold.

He said again, "Could we dispense with the ghoulish conversation, I want to enjoy my dinner. Ray, I have to use your toaster oven, this slice is cold."

I replied, "Wait, I think everyone's slice is cold. I'll put them on a sheet and put them in the oven."

After we finished our dinner, Delores and Don left.

When they were gone Sue asked, "Was it necessary to tell Delores about our séance? I thought we agreed to keep it to ourselves."

"Why? Don't you want Delores in on what's happening? You've been involved in séances together before. You're supposed to be good friends."

She sternly remarked, "I'd rather her not be involved in this. That's the way I want it. Ok?"

I countered her stern verbal lashing, "Well, my remark slipped out. I'm sorry."

She looked at me as if she could tell I was lying. I let it go at that, and helped her with her coat. After sliding it over her shoulders I went to embrace her, but she quickly pulled away. Was I losing her to whatever forces were pulling her in a different direction?

I asked, "Sue, I'll have to pack a few clothes if I'm staying at your house. I won't be a min__."

She didn't give me a chance to finish before replying, "That's ok. I don't think it's necessary for you to stay over. For some reason, I don't feel frightened any longer."

"Are you sure? You seemed to be really afraid to be left alone last night?"

"Yes, I'm sure. I must have sounded foolish."

I didn't like her answer. Was it about the conversation she had with Justin while they were having lunch, or was it what we uncovered tonight in front of Delores and Don?

Pulling into her driveway, I was about to get out of the car thinking I could stay awhile, when she suddenly turned and said, "No Ray, I'd rather be alone tonight."

She read my mind again, and I replied, "If you have any problem tonight, don't hesitate to call. Should I call you tomorrow?"

"Why don't you wait till I call you, I may just decide to sleep late."

With nothing else to counter her brush off, I replied, "Then I'll wait for your call."

I waited until she was in the house, and the living room lights went on, before backing out of the driveway.

Getting to my apartment door, I could hear my phone ringing. Quickly unlocking the door, I grabbed the phone hoping it was Susan changing her mind about me staying. I was disappointed to hear Delores's voice.

"Ray, I want to warn you. Something's not right with Sue. She's acting very strange. Is she still there?"

"No, she wanted me to take her home shortly after you left. Last night she was frightened to death to be alone, and tonight when I dropped her off, she didn't want me to come in. What do you make of it?"

"I don't know, but whatever it is, it has nothing to do with the blue bottle. That's only the doorway to whatever's happening. I seriously think she's dealing with a world of spirits. When you said there were no marks in the snow outside her window after you saw the shadow. That confirms to me you're dealing with spirits. I think I'll call her just to make sure she's alright."

"Thanks Delores. Call me after you're done and let me know what she says."

"I will."

I mixed a little stiffer drink than when Don was here, and sat in the living room to ponder what Delores told me. It didn't sound encouraging at all, and I'm sure the innocence of George willing Sue the bottle and dressing bureau, would have come into question, had he knew what was taking place. Still, I wondered how I could break the tentacles of a past that was slowly pulling Susan down. Would I lose this battle? I began to relax, closing my eyes for what seemed like a few moments when the phone rang.

"Hello, who's calling?"

"It's Delores," continuing excitedly. "I've been trying to call Sue but she doesn't answer. Are you sure she didn't go out again?"

Hearing her words I sat up. "I don't think so. She said she was pretty tired."

"How long has it been since you dropped her off?"

Looking at my watch, I was surprised. I must have made my mixed drink stronger than I thought. It was already more than an hour ago. I replied, "I dropped her off a little more than an hour ago, why?"

"Look Ray, not to upset you, but I have a bad feeling about this. I have a key to her house. Why don't you pick me up and we'll go over and see if she's ok?"

Jumping up from the sofa responding to her being alarmed, I said, "I'm putting on my coat now. I'll see you in about 15 minutes."

Pulling up in front of Delores', both her and Don, came out to the car. After getting in, I hurriedly drove the distance to Sue's. Turning the corner into Sue's street, I almost careened out of control on a patch of ice. After recovering, I hurriedly pulled into the driveway next to her car. I paused for a moment then said to Delores and Don, "I wonder why she pulled the car out of the garage?"

Don asked, "Wasn't it outside when you dropped her off?"

"No, it was inside."

Don replied, "Maybe she wanted to go out for something and changed her mind."

Delores replied, "I know Sue too well. She would have never left it outside. She would have put it back in the garage."

We got out and I noticed the windows on the garage door were covered with a sheet. I found a small opening at the corner of one window and peered into the darkness. The lights were off in the house, and I was about to walk around to examine each window, when Delores excitedly waved to me. I hurried to her and asked, "What is it?"

"Come around this side of the house. It's Sue's bedroom window."

I followed her and through a small opening at the bottom of the shade, I could see a dimly lit set of candles. They were the same candlesticks she brought out from her bedroom, when Delores and Don came to dinner. They were separated by what appeared to be a folder. Suddenly my focus went from the candles to movement in the room. I looked in horror at what appeared to be someone robed, sitting on the bench seat reading it. We didn't notice at first, but scanning the candle lit room, we could see several other robed people surrounding her bed.

"Delores, what the hell do you think this is all about?"

"It looks like the vision I had when I put myself in a trance after Don and I went home. I knew something was wrong, and the only way to find out was to do it."

"You mean you actually saw this gathering?"

"Yes, when Sue mentioned the old woman, I conjured up a vision in my mind of what she might look like. Suddenly, the robed person who was reading turned toward the few standing around Sue's bed. She looked old and haggard.

Delores said as she was examining what was taking place, "I guess I was right. Look at the person sitting on the bench at the dressing bureau. She's looks like she's reading while she's brushing out her long blond hair. Just the way George described his grandmother."

A sudden chill went up my spine, and it wasn't from the cold or standing in the snow. This scene was a sequel to any horror movie I could think of about the occult. Don, wondering where we were, came around the house.

"Hey, you guys, what gives. Are you two becoming peeping Tom's?"

Delores put her finger to her lips and said quietly, "Shush!" But his voice was loud enough for the people inside to hear. I observed what seemed to be the leader look in our direction, then motioned the others to leave. The procession filed out of the room for the exception of the person that seemed to be the leader. He took off his robe and to my surprise, it was Justin. The old woman sitting at the dresser seemed to be vaporizing, slowly being absorbed into the mirror.

I frantically said, "Where's Susan?"

I had enough of this shock, and against Delores' wishes, rushed around to the front door. I rang the doorbell then proceeded to pound on the door with my fist. Don and Delores were trying to calm me down, but I was too fearful not knowing what dangers Susan might be in.

Delores pleadingly said, "Ray, try not to be upset with Susan. She may not know this was even happening. Give her a chance to tell us what went on."

I looked at her, realizing she was right I forcefully had to subdue my anger. A few moments later, the outside light went on and the door opened. Sue was standing there in her white bath robe wiping her eyes, as though she had just awoke from a sound sleep.

I said in a loud tone, "Sue, what the hell's going on in here?"

Delores pulled on my coat sleeve in a manner reminding me to keep calm.

Susan replied, "What do you mean, by that? What's going on here? I told you I was going to bed early." Looking past me still appearing to be still half asleep she asked, "What's this all about Delores?"

"We tried calling several times, but you didn't answer. We were wondering whether you were all right. Can we come in?"

Still looking sleepy, she stepped aside, "Certainly. Come in, come in."

Upon entering, I took a quick scan around the room and from what I could see, there was no one present.

I asked, "Sue, are you here alone?"

She looked mystified at my question, and I repeated myself, "Are you al__." I didn't have a chance to finish before Delores interrupted.

"We thought we saw movement in the house, that's why he asked."

"Who would be here when I'm sleeping?"

Delores quickly thought to ask, "Sue, I forgot to tell you. I have a séance tomorrow night. I wondered if you would let me use the bottle. May I?"

"Certainly, I'll get it."

Delores quickly followed her into the bedroom, and suddenly there was a scream. Don and I rushed to the bedroom to see Delores passed out on the floor. Bending down to assist her, we saw the image of a woman in the reflection of the mirror. She was sitting on the bench seat brushing out her long hair, but in reality the seat was empty. From the light of the candles still burning, the woman slowly turned. Her face was wrinkled with age, and had a horrid expression, then slowly broke into a half smile. We could see the faint images of a Confederate soldier and a Revolutionary War soldier in the background, slowly disappearing.

Could they be the two that Susan saw rising from the dead? Were they sentries guarding something, the old woman perhaps? Was that the reason she was smiling? Knowing she was secure with her bodyguards?

Don was helping Delores recover, while Sue just looked on, not offering any assistance. I thought it strange she didn't assist. I blew out the candles and the images in the mirror slowly faded away.

Taking Delores by the arm, Don helped her to the living room sofa. I got a glass of water from the refrigerator and handed it to her.

"Here Delores, have a few sips of this."

I turned to look at Sue who seemed to be just recognizing our presence. She asked, "What are you doing here? Who let you in?"

"Sue, you let us in. Don't you remember?" I said.

"The last thing I remember was getting extremely tired. I felt like I hadn't slept for days and went to bed. I had the strangest dream. I dreamt I was in bed and there was a circle of people wearing robes standing around me. Then for some reason I woke up. You say I answered the door?"

"Yes. I think you may be in danger. Suppose I stay the night?"

"Delores interjected in a commanding voice, letting Sue know she didn't have any options, "I think you should come home with us, or go with Ray. It's not safe to stay here tonight."

"Why isn't it? It was just a bad dream," Sue replied.

While they were discussing Sue's problem, I slipped away checking every room and closet in the house for people. There was no one there. The house was empty for the exception of us four. Returning to the living room, I backed Delores's suggestion.

"I think you should do what Delores says. I'll help you get a few things together.

Delores remarked, "That's Ok Ray, I'll help her. Come on, Sue."

Before going into the bedroom, Don took Delores by the arm and said, "I'm coming with you in case you have another passing out episode."

I had the same idea, and we all went in.

Entering the room, it was as though nothing had occurred. But wait! Where's the leather bound folder that was here. It didn't disappear by itself. I thought, "Maybe the old woman took it with her." After Delores helped her pack a few things, she walked Sue out to my car. Don and I took one last look around the house before I closed the door, and locked it.

$$\mathcal{C}hapter\ 9$$

On the way to Don's, I asked Sue, "Do you want to stay at Delores', or come home with me?

Don quickly replied, "Why don't you both stay with us: we have three bedrooms?"

Susan still looked a little confused as to why she was being shuffled off from the comfort of her own home. As if she was being kidnapped by strangers, she suddenly asked, "Where are you taking me?"

Looking at her, I realized she was in more of a transcendental state than we ever imagined. Did they give her some sort of potion to make her think it was a dream? What sort of ritual were they about to have before we interrupted? If Delores didn't have the psychic ability she has, we wouldn't have known she was in danger. I answered, "Sue, you've been through a horrible experience. Do you remember drinking anything while you were dreaming?"

Pausing to think, she said, "Yes, I remember. It's all misty, but I seemed to have been walking through the woods and came into a small clearing, where I saw a log cabin. There was an old woman sitting in a rocking chair on the front porch, smoking a corn cob pipe, reading from a brown leather bound folder. As I approached to ask her for directions, she stood up inviting me inside for a cool drink of water," Sue paused for a moment wringing her hands together, trying to remember, then continued. "It's funny."

"What's funny?" I replied.

"She seemed to know what I wanted before I asked. I followed her inside the cabin, and she went to the kitchen. I kept asking her where I was, but she didn't answer. She led me to the kitchen sink where there was an old-fashioned hand water pump. She began pumping the handle up and down until the water came out. she invited me to put my hand under the spout. I kept asking her for directions home, but she wouldn't answer my question. She just kept urging me to put my hand under the spout and feel the cool water. After I let the water flow over my hand, she took a glass off the shelf and began to fill it. I remember her saying as she handed me the glass of water, 'This will make you feel better.' After I took a few sips, she seemed to have a satisfied look on her face and I didn't feel anxious to find my way home any longer."

We realized the glass of water she was given to drink, must have been the potion to put her in a state of suspended animation.

I asked, "Sue was anyone else in the cabin?"

"I didn't see anyone, but I remember looking around, and seeing what looked like a Revolutionary War soldier's uniform hanging over a chair."

Delores asked, "Did you happen to see any Confederate soldiers uniform?"

"No: just the Revolutionary War clothes. Why?"

I looked at Delores, and realized we had the same thought in mind. The period Sue was wandering through had to be before the civil war. I asked, "Then what happened?"

Delores cut me off, "Ray, I think maybe we should all stay at my house. We can discuss this after Sue gets a shower."

I took the hint. Delores wanted to discuss what we just learned while Sue was getting ready for bed, so I kept quiet.

Arriving at Don's, I carried Sue's bag to the bedroom where she would sleep. I heard Delores say, "Here, Sue, you can use this robe.

Why don't you take a nice hot shower?"

"I think I'll take a nice hot bath instead, if you don't mind?" she replied.

After Susan went into the bathroom and began filling the tub, Delores, Don and I went to the kitchen. I asked, "Delores, that cool drink of water the old woman gave her, could that be the potion to make her believe she was really dreaming?"

"Yes. The whole picture in her mind was a deception of imagining she was thirsty. People trying to control you, put you in that state of mind. They want to be seen as being helpful."

"You mean by offering her the drink of cool water?"

"That's it; exactly. Remember, Sue never said she was thirsty, it was a suggestion from the old woman."

Don asked, "Sue mentioned the Revolutionary War uniform. Could she be back farther in time than that?"

Delores replied, "We'll have to try having a séance ourselves to find out. I have the blue bottle with me."

I replied, "I think it's kind of late tonight, how about having it tomorrow evening?"

Delores appeared to be thinking about my statement, replying, "Ray, I have a suggestion. Do you think it's possible if we could go back to George's and have the séance?"

"All the way up there?" Don exclaimed.

"Yes. It might be better if we can have it in the blue bottle's natural environment."

Don asked, "Delores, you're not suggesting we haul the dresser back up are you?"

"No, just the bottle."

I replied, "I'll have to call Frank and ask if he still has access to George's house, and whether there is still a table and chairs. I can also ask what the weather conditions are. Where's your telephone?"

"It's in the living__" stopping short, Delores quietly added hearing Susan leaving the bathroom, "Use the telephone in my bedroom."

Taking the phone number from my wallet, I dialed Frank's number.

"Hello, Frank, this is Ray Bishop. I was wondering whether you have a lot of snow up there?"

He replied, "We probably didn't get as much as you, only about two and it's just about gone. Why?"

"We were thinking about running up in the morning. Do you still have access to George's house?"

"Yes, I still have the keys. We haven't made a decision on the house yet. There's an Amish family that's interested, that is, if it's still available in the spring. I think that'll be the best bet. They really don't care what the house looks like inside, they generally gut out the plumbing and electricity anyway. Why are you asking?"

"I hate to bring this up, but that blue bottle and dresser we brought down are creating a problem." Before I had a chance to continue, there was a moment of silence.

He finally asked, "What kind of problem?"

"I can explain it to you when we get there. Are the kitchen table and chairs still there?"

"Yes, everything's pretty much the way we left it when you were here."

"Good! We'll probably be up before noon tomorrow. Thanks Frank."

Hanging up the phone, I returned to the living room.

"Delores, I told Frank we'd be there around noon tomorrow, is that alright with you and Don?"

"Yes, that's fine."

Susan was joining us in the kitchen, when she heard me speaking about Frank, "Whoa! Whoa, wait a minute. Go. Go where?" she asked.

Delores, looking sternly at Sue replied, "We're going back to George's farm and having a séance. I want to find out why you're being targeted for what took place tonight. Ray called Frank, and he said the roads are clear. Most of the furniture at George's is still there, so it shouldn't be a problem having one."

A temporary look of resentment on Sue's face was quickly replaced by a smile of satisfaction by Delores's concern. Embracing Delores, Susan said, "Thanks Dee."

With that comment, I said, "I don't know about all of you, but I'm going to bed. We have a long drive in the morning."

Don replied, "I think that's a good idea. I'll set the alarm for 6:00. Good night all."

***

For some reason, I had a difficult time falling asleep, but woke before anyone else. Going from my bedroom, I put my ear to Susan's door, but didn't hear her stirring. Making my way to the kitchen by the aid of night lights, I was passing the living room, when I noticed a faint blue glow coming from the coffee table. Curious as to what the soft blue light was, I entered the room. It seemed to be radiating from the blue bottle. I picked it up and could see for the first time, what Sue and Delores was talking about. The mist effect in the bottle made the light emanating from it appear to be pulsating, from bright to dim, then back again. I looked at it for a few minutes before realizing I was being captivated by its mysterious glow, and quickly put it down.

I was about to awaken the others, when I looked at my watch, it was only 5:15. I didn't want to disturb anyone else at this hour, and continued to the kitchen to put on the coffee. Periodically, as I was making it, I glanced out at the living room and could see the soft glow from the bottle. I thought, "Why didn't it do that last evening? Is it reenergizing itself? Who's controlling it?" All these questions were going through my mind.

Returning to the living room, I gazed into the mist, and could see a circle of hooded people repeating words from who appeared to be the leader. He was standing in the center of the circle, reading from what looked like the same brown leather bound folder that was on Susan's bureau. The one that disappeared after the old woman and the two soldiers faded into the mirror. It was missing after our intrusion at Susan's. Could it have been taken back with the disappearing spirits?

I was afraid of what I was allowed to see from the mist, and wondered why I was all of a sudden privileged to be able to do it. My first thought, was anger towards an inanimate object, and wanted to destroy something that was getting between Susan and me. If it wasn't for my strong attachment with her, I would have just as soon dumped it in the ocean. After refocusing on the bottle, it seemed like the mist would appear, then fade. It focused on a scene where the leader stopped reading, and three people entered the circle. The one in the center appeared to be a woman being escorted by a man on each side. Approaching the leader, they let go of the woman's arms. The leader then handed the folder to her, and joined the others as part of the circle. I looked in horror as the hooded woman turned and took down her hood. Was I imagining things? It was the spitting image of Susan. So engrossed in watching, I was startled when I heard the alarm go off in Don's room. I turned on the living room lamp just as he stepped from his bedroom.

"Good morning Ray. You're up early."

"Yes, I didn't get much sleep last night. I put on the coffee when I got up though, I hope you don't mind?"

"Don't mind? Hell no! It smells good. Delores will be right out, she's showering. I know she'll appreciate it. Is Susan up yet?" he asked.

"I don't know. I'll knock at her door."

I listened at her door for a few moments, and just as I was ready to knock, the door opened.

"Good morning, Sue! The coffee's on. Shall I bring you a cup?" I said.

"That's ok. I'll come out in a few minutes. I just want to brush my hair."

"Would you like me to make you some toast?"

"Toast will be fine, but you don't have to make it. I can do it myself."

"Whatever you say, I'll be in the kitchen with Don."

I returned to the kitchen in time to hear Don ask Delores, "I wonder whether we'll find out anymore about this group that seems to want Susan in their midst with a séance?"

Looking in my direction as I entered the kitchen, I said, "I don't know Don, but we're sure as hell going to try."

I was standing in the entrance with my hand against the wall when Sue came up behind me. Putting her arms around my waist, she repeated my words, "Sure as hell going to try what?"

"Don was asking whether we'll find out more about this group that seems to want to pull you in."

She replied, "Why go all the way up to George'. Why not have it right here?"

I was at a loss for words, but Delores came to my rescue, "We thought it might be better having it there. Maybe the spirits that are within the bottle, have some connection with George's house. He did say it was where his grandmother and great grandmother lived. Maybe that's significant."

After finishing our coffee, Delores wrapped the blue bottle in a heavy towel, and placed it in her canvass bag along with a few candles. After taking a last look around the living room to make sure we didn't leave anything, we headed out for the farm.

The drive was filled with conversation about how spirits could manifest themselves as real flesh and bones, and at will, vanish without a trace, not leaving as much as a footprint in the snow. If an outsider were riding with us listening to our conversation, our group would have wound up in the parking lot of a mental institution, instead of our intended destination.

We were coming off the turnpike around 10:00. With money and the toll ticket in hand, I opened my window letting the cold air rush in. As I handed it to the toll collector, I saw he was an older person. I asked, "How's the weather been up here?"

After getting up from his stool and stretching, he covered a yawn with his fist replying, "Not too bad. We had a few inches the other day, but it didn't last long. It's unusual that were having so little snow. When I was a kid, we'd probably have about a foot on the ground by Thanksgiving, and wouldn't see the ground again until spring."

I thought to myself, "Here we go again, with when I was a kid, things were harsher." I almost expected him to say, "We had to fight our way a mile to school through snow drifts six feet high, uphill- both ways." I smiled as he handed me my change, happy he couldn't read my thoughts.

"Have a nice day," I said, then quickly rolled up the window and drove away.

I noticed the trees were almost completely bare, for the exception of a few brown leaves on some of the oaks. Their stubbornness to let go of autumn, would be challenged by the coming of harsher winds, and driving snows in the impending winter ahead.

"Don, I think we should check in at the motel first. I'll call Frank from there, and see if we can meet him at George's. What do you think?"

Delores chimed in, "I think that's a great idea as long as we can have lunch somewhere first."

"How about the Chatterbox?" I replied.

"Chatterbox it is."

While we were checking in, the clerk asked, "Will that be two rooms?"

Don looked at me to answer, and in turn I looked at Sue. She said to my surprise, "Two rooms."

I didn't want to seem overly excited by her answer, but couldn't contain my smile as Delores gave me a look of approval. Even Don noticed my upbeat response of being a little nervous, until Susan remarked, "As long as the room has two beds."

Feeling a little flustered I excused myself saying, "I think I'll call Frank."

Don replied, "You do that. I'll bring the bags from the car,"

"Why don't you wait until I call Frank, then I'll help you? Sue why don't you go up to the room, I'll be there shortly."

Delores and Sue headed for the room, and I went to the telephone.

"Hello Frank! This is Ray. We're in Wysox checking in at the motel. What time shall we meet you at George's?"

He replied, "Did you want to check the place out first? There's only a wood stove there and it hasn't been lit since we left."

"I think that may be a good idea. We're kind of hungry. We were thinking about going to the Chatterbox. Would you and June care to join us?"

I could hear the muffled sound of his voice probably holding the phone to his chest, "June, Ray's on the phone. He asks if we want to join him and__, he stopped the conversation with June for a moment and asked. Who else is with you?"

I replied, "Don, Delores and Sue."

I could hear him continue telling June what I said, "Don, Delores and Sue. Do you want to go?"

I could hear her reply, "Yes, what time?"

He got back to me, "What time?"

"We're checked in." looking at my watch I continued, "It's 11:30 now, how about if we meet you there at 12:15?"

"Ok, we'll be there."

It was the first time he joined me for an invitation to breakfast or lunch, and I almost felt honored at his accepting my offer. I felt as though the ice had really been broken as strangers, and was looking forward to a complete acceptance as a friend.

When we arrived at the Chatterbox Parking Lot, I noticed Frank's truck was already there. Crossing the street and entering the establishment, we saw Frank and June talking to people they obviously knew. When they saw us, they waved for us to join them. Nodding at the people sitting at the table, June introduced us, "Jody, Edgar, this is Ray Bishop, the guy that bought Frank's mother and father's place. These are his friends from the city. Delores, and her husband Don, and this is Susan," pausing, "I think she's Ray's girlfriend, but I'm not really sure."

Sue smiled, realizing I was waiting for her to answer, she said, "I guess she's right."

Frank added, "Edgar and Jody as well as the rest of this crowd, we all went to school together."

"Glad to make your acquaintance," I said.

After our introduction and a few words in exchange, we found an empty table for 6 and sat down. Ruthie, the waitress came to our table, and with the same friendly home spun manner, she said, "Howdy, June, Frank. I see Ray's got you two involved in his project. How are you folks today?"

I replied, "We're fine Ruthie. What's for lunch?"

She humorously replied looking over her shoulder toward the kitchen.

"Well, if the cook can catch up to that beef critter running around back there, hamburger deluxe is the special for today. That comes with fries and slaw. The pickle is where we really tack on the extra charge."

Laughing at her humor, we placed our order.

I couldn't help but notice a few of the patrons sitting at Jody and Edgar's table staring in our direction. I felt certain June must have mentioned the séances to Jody. Did they think we were weird? I wasn't sure, so I asked Frank, "Did you or June by chance, happen to mention the séances to your friends?"

"Yes. Why?" June replied.

"They seem to be fixated on our table. They don't think we're kooky, do you?"

"No, they don't. In fact, you're a little famous."

"How's that?" I asked.

June replied, "When I told them what went on at the house, they thought it would make for a great book." June laughed adding, "Jody asked whether we should put it under fiction or science."

Our food came to the table, and as usual, it was more than a generous proportion. The whole time I was eating, I could feel the eyes of everyone in the room watching us.

"Frank, you said you haven't been there since we left with the dresser, I__" I didn't get a chance to finish, before June excitedly asked, "Are we going to have a séance tonight?"

Delores replied, "Yes. That's why we're here. It seems that the dressing bureau and blue bottle are giving Sue a problem."

"What kind of problem?" June asked.

"She seems to be getting drawn into a group of people. She doesn't, or rather we don't, understand what they want."

Frank replied, "Well, we don't have the dresser."

"I know, but we have the blue bottle. Maybe we can find out why it's doing what it's doing. Or what she's supposed to do."

After lunch we followed Frank to George's farm. Pulling up to the back porch, even before we went inside, the house seemed strangely empty. Although it was winter, I could still envision George sitting on his back porch sorting apples, the way he was the day I met him.

"It feels so sad coming back here, the house seems so empty," Sue said.

I turned to look at her, "Those were the exact words I was thinking. Did you read my mind?"

Delores answered, "Probably, I felt the same thing."

I felt naked but didn't elaborate.

Exiting the car, we walked up the stone path to the back porch. Taking out the key, Frank unlocked the door and we went in. He was right. The house had the damp coldness of not having a friendly fire for weeks.

"Frank, should I light a fire in the stove?" I asked.

"It might not be a good idea unless we intend to stay. I wouldn't want to burn the house down."

Sue said, "It's already 3:00 o'clock. I don't see any reason to run back to the motel, it'll be dark in about 2 hours, why not just stay."

"I think you're right. I'll build the fire. Don, you and Delores can set the chairs around the table. I only see four, we'll have to look around the house and see if we can find two more."

Before Susan walked away in search of the chairs, June said, "Sue, you don't have to look. Frank and I brought two of ours. They're in the back of the truck. Let's go get'em.'"

I walked out on the porch, and picked up an old newspaper from the pile being held in place by a brick, and brought in a few pieces of kindling. I opened the pot- belly stove and crumpled up the newspaper and put it in the bottom, and carefully stacked the kindling over it. I found matches in the end table drawer where I left them. I struck the match and put it to the paper lighting my creation. The fire quickly spread and soon caught onto a few pieces of wood chips. The flames spread along the fibers of the dry kindling, creating smoke, and I immediately knew the seasoned wood was hickory. The smell alone, made the room feel comfortable, even without the full benefit of warmth. In a few minutes, I added a few more pieces of wood before closing the door.

June and Sue came back to the kitchen with the extra chairs, placing them around the table. Delores placed the candles at different points of the room, while Sue went to George's desk to get a pencil and paper. She remembered they were in the desk from George asking her to get a pencil and paper, when he willed her the dressing bureau. It was actually a combination of a writing desk with a pull-down front, with shelves above, accessed by wood and glass doors. While she was routing through a drawer, she suddenly looked up then screamed. Don and I rushed to the living room.

"What is it? What's happened Sue?"

She was visibly shaken then said, "I was routing through the drawer for a pencil, and when I looked up. I saw George's reflection in the glass! He was smiling at me."

A sudden chill went up my spine, and I'm sure Don felt the same. We looked at each other, with probably the same thought in mind. We came here to find a resolve, not have a bigger problem.

"Why don't we begin the séance?" I suggested.

Don and Fred replied at exactly the same second, "Good idea!"

Delores took the blue bottle and laid it on its side in the center of the table, and Sue placed the small pieces of paper with *YES* and *NO* at each end.

After everyone took seats, I lit the candles and turned out the light. Returning to my seat, we held hands around the table, suspiciously eyeing each other not knowing what this meeting would produce. Delores and Sue lowered their heads relaxing, getting ready to accept whatever spirit was present.

Secretly, I was hoping for George's grandmother, or great grandmother to come forward, but since we saw the log cabin in George's great grandmother's time, I assumed we would only be able to contact her.

It was a familiar scene, reminiscent of the séances of a few short months ago at my farm. Hopefully we wouldn't be joined by anyone like Daniel's angry spirit.

At the moment the spirit entered Delores's body, her hair fluffed up, and we knew she was able to accept questions.

June asked, "Is there a spirit present?"

The bottle slowly turned, pointing to the word *YES*.

Delores raised her head and opened her eyes. Staring straight ahead into the candle lit room she answered, "Yes, it's me."

June asked, "Are you George's grandmother?"

The silence was broken by laughter from someone outside Delores. I quickly asked, "Is George there with you?"

The bottle slowly turned to the word *YES*, and the voice quietly spoke, "Yes, he's one of us now."

"What do you mean by one of us?" June asked.

The voice broke into laughter again, and I quickly asked, "Can he come forward to answer questions?"

Before the bottle had a chance to turn, a voice replied, "Ray, I'm here."

I recognized the voice, but with the strange laughter, I lost my attention to the other people sitting at the table. I was surprised the voice was coming from Don. I wondered why Delores was the only person speaking, when I distinctly saw Sue's hair fluff at the same moment. Was she possessed by someone of authority that only spoke when necessary? I didn't know, but I decided to ask.

"To the spirit that's within Susan, are you someone that's in control?"

The voice laughed again, but without Susan moving, it didn't indicate it was coming from her.

I asked, "Why is Susan being troubled by the spirits in the dressing bureau and the blue bottle?"

Delores opened her eyes again and laughed, joining the other laughter from whoever it was in the room.

I demanded, "George, you manifested yourself in the glass at the desk to Susan. Were you trying to contact her?"

Don looked in my direction smiling, "Yes, I want to warn her__."

Sue slowly turned looking at Don, and I was certain George was cut off by the power of whoever possessed Susan. I pressed the question adamantly again raising my voice, "George, answer me! Warn her about what?"

The bottle began to glow as it did on Don's coffee table. I stood it upright and the mist grew brighter then turned back the pages of history once again. I looked at Frank and June. They were as mesmerized as me, watching the history of George's family's past. I began to realize the blue bottle wasn't only his great grandmother's. Its history went back to Europe centuries ago.

Wide-eyed, Frank remarked, "I remember seeing in the Bradford County Library, the record of the original settlers that came here, some were from England and some were from Scotland. Maybe that's how we're able to see that place we're looking at?"

I replied, "Frank, that's Stonehenge. It's a place where a cult used to practice some sort of religion."

Saying that brought another laugh, and finally a response from Susan, "I have to go back. That's where I belong."

I angrily demanded, "You're not Susan! Why does she have to go back?"

She slowly turned looking in my direction and said, "She's the chosen one."

I raised my voice even louder, demanding, "Chosen. Chosen for what? She's not dead like you, she's alive. Alive! Do you hear me?"

There was loud laughter at my helpless triad, then the blue bottle began to grow dim. Finally as if its last bit of energy was used, it went out. The mist was no longer visible, and Delores and Sue began returning to normal.

Delores asked, "What did you find out?"

"We still haven't found out who's in control, but whoever it is, they said Sue's the chosen one."

Sue asked, "Chosen? Chosen for what?"

"I don't know, but I don't like it. It may be dangerous to you. I think on the way home, we should throw this damn bottle in the Susquehanna River."

Delores replied, "I don't think we should do that. There's something powerful going on, and I believe the bottle is a doorway to whatever it is we're trying to figure out. No, that's a bad idea."

June asked, "I wonder, if George can hear us, maybe he could occupy the bottle and help us solve it."

Frank asked, "Did anyone ever notice whether George was ever in any of the scenes in the mist?"

Susan thought for a moment, and replied, "Yes, I saw an image of a small boy sitting on the floor watching his grandmother, brushing out her long hair. I remember him telling me she would say strange words he couldn't understand."

Delores quickly added, "Then that's all we have to do when we go back to the city. Have another séance and ask George to come forward."

We agreed to keep the bottle and prepared to leave. I made sure the fire was almost extinguished before exiting the house. Stepping out on the back porch, the air was cold and a few flakes began to fall.

I said, "Frank, I thought you said they didn't predict snow?"

"They didn't. Don't get nervous. Sometime the mist coming off the mountain freezes with the cold air, and creates a few flakes. It's nothing to worry about though."

After Frank locked the door, we said goodnight parting in different directions.

Chapter 10

Getting back to the motel, I wasn't quite sure how to handle the situation, being in the same room with Sue. After the séance this evening, my mind wasn't totally on enjoying a first experience with her. Too much had taken place, and my concern for a long term future relationship, meant more than my own personal satisfaction. After saying goodnight to Delores and Don, we entered the room.

"Look, Sue, I don't want you to think I'm a prude, but with what happened tonight, don't feel that you have to be pressured by something you said when we checked in- I understand."

She came close and caressed my face, giving me a light peck on the lips.

"I knew you would understand. There's a desire inside me that wants to experience you, but every time I feel it, there's a force that seems to be blocking that emotion. I know it isn't me. It's something, or someone doing it. That's the best I can explain it."

"You mean, like trying to possess your spirit?"

"I guess that's a way you can describe it. In all these years I've been giving readings, and séances, I've never experienced this. It's really got me scared."

She quickly turned away, covering her face with open hands, and began to cry. I stepped close behind her, putting my arms around her waist.

"Don't worry Sue, we'll figure it out. Try not to let it upset you."

Turning around to face me, we kissed, and I think that helped temporarily. Looking down at her face, I wiped the tears from her eyes then kissed the end of her nose.

"Maybe you should relax in a hot tub for awhile, that might be just what you need," I suggested.

"You're right. But why don't you take a shower first? I'll probably soak for a good half hour."

"Ok!"

Going through my bag, I found a set of underwear and pajama bottoms. Pulling them from the bag Susan laughed. Looking at her I asked, "What's so funny?"

She replied, "Did you think I would mind if you slept in your underclothes?"

"No, I sleep with pajamas on every night during the winter months," humorously continuing, "I'm just glad I didn't bring my teddy bear set. Now that would have been embarrassing."

She laughed, "You really have a teddy bear set?"

Looking down at my pajamas I laughed, "Yes, it must be a security thing from when I was a kid."

After showering I went back to the bedroom. Sue took her personal items and quickly exchanged places. I could hear the bath tub filling, and could picture her sliding into the warm water. Not to get myself too aroused, I turned on the TV. As she predicted, within a half hour she returned to the bedroom. Looking at her with the towel around her wet hair, and heavy robe on, she still looked desirable enough for me to abandon my commitment of celibacy.

"You look like a swami with that towel around your hair."

She smiled, "Promise me you won't laugh?"

"Why would I laugh?"

She turned away from me and unfastened her robe belt. Quickly turning around she threw open her robe. To my surprise, she was wearing pajamas with hearts and cupids. I laughed, "Now we're even," I said.

She replied, "I guess we are."

"Which side of the bed do you like to sleep on?" I asked, pointing to the bed I was lying on.

She replied smiling, "I think I'll take the bed on the right."

I waited until she slid under her covers, then turned out the light. "Good night, Sue. Sweet dreams."

"Thanks! you too!"

I lie awake for a half hour before finally drifting off to sleep. Not long after I fell asleep, I awoke to Sue talking. I rose up on my elbow, and looked at the clock on the bedside cabinet. It was 3:30 a.m.

"Sue, are you alright?"

She was facing away from me in the fetal position, and didn't answer. I couldn't make it out clearly, but it sounded as if she was pleading with someone not to have to go with them. I turned on the small reading lamp and asked again. Still, there was no response. I got out of bed and shook her shoulder.

"Sue, wake up!"

She slowly turned, giving me a look of someone that didn't want to be disturbed, a frightening look, a look of someone that wanted me to pay a price for my unwanted intrusion.

I shook her shoulder again, "Sue, wake up!"

When I turned on a brighter light, I could see she was drenched in sweat. She began to slowly get back her senses, by rubbing her eyes and shaking her head.

"What happened?" she asked.

"You must have had a bad dream. You were pleading with someone."

"Pleading for what?" she replied.

"It sounded like someone wanted you to go with them, but you were refusing. That's what it sounded like. That towel around your head is soaked with sweat. Let me get you a dry one and a drink of water."

Returning to her bedside, my foot accidently hit something. I thought at first it was one of her shoes, but when I looked down, it was the blue bottle. I asked. "Sue, were you using the blue bottle while I was asleep?"

"Why?" she asked.

Picking it up, I sat down on the edge of her bed then held it up, "This is why. I don't think you should be bothering this thing when there's no one else around."

Again, she gave me the same disturbed look at my unwanted opinion.

"I'll be fine with it. I don't know why it's at my bedside. I left it in my overnight bag. I must have sleep walked and put it there, but I don't remember doing it."

I put the bottle back in her bag, turned out the light, and got back into bed. "Just remember what I'm telling you. I'd leave it alone."

***

I awoke to Susan already up and dressed. Wiping my eyes then yawning, I said, "Good morning. How did you sleep the rest of the night?"

"I slept just fine. I'll go down to the cafeteria and bring you back a coffee."

"That sounds great. In the meantime I'll take a shower."

After she left the room, I got out of bed. I looked at the dresser and my eyes caught a glimpse of something. My immediate feeling was anger Sue disregarded my warning from last night. There stood prominently was the blue bottle. Picking it up, I curiously looked at it, remembering I put it in her bag before going back to bed during the night. I thought, "I know I did. Why is it back out of her bag? Has she been playing around with this again?" Shaking my head as I went into the bathroom I thought, "She obviously didn't heed my warning, and put it back in her bag."

After I showered, I came out to the smell of a fresh cup of coffee.

"That smells good Sue. Do you know if Delores and Don are up?"

Looking in the mirror adjusting her hair she replied, "Delores is already eating breakfast, Don should be down soon. I think I'll go back and join her."

"That sounds like a good idea, I'll be there shortly."

Stepping out in the hall, I met Don coming out of his room. Giving me a wink, he said, "Hi Ray, how did things go last night?"

"Not so well," I replied.

"Why? I thought you two hit it off pretty good."

"We never became amorous if that's what you're thinking. She became captivated by that damned blue bottle again. I woke up to her pleading with someone not to take her. It must have been a terrible dream, she was soaked with sweat."

He was about to question me further just as the elevator doors opened, and I was happy not to have to continue the conversation.

Entering the dining room we got our food and joined the girls.

Delores remarked, "Ray, I hear you had to assist Susan during the night. She said she was glad you were there to help."

I was happy Susan decided to tell her about the experience. Every time we talked about it in a group, we always seemed to learn more.

"Yes, Delores, it was a little scary."

After some conversation about what went on, we finished breakfast, then checked out.

Continuing the discussion on the drive back to the city, neither of us had any resolve to Sue's dilemma. We did come to the conclusion the bottle has to be the doorway to whatever's pulling Susan in, but what to do about it, was another question. Who, or whatever it might be, will have to be dealt with sooner or later.

With the city coming into view, it wasn't long before I dropped Delores and Don at their house.

"Thanks for coming you guys. Don, I'll call you later in the week."

Delores added, "If anything changes Sue, give me a call."

"I will, but I don't think it will be necessary."

Pulling away from the curb I said, "Sue, do you mean what you said about calling Delores if anything changes?"

She didn't answer and kept looking out the passenger window. Repeating my words, she slowly turned, and her eyes took on a look of disinterest. Trying to concentrate on my driving and look at her at the same time, I said, "I'm not a psychic, but I can tell by the look on your face, you don't intend to let Delores in on your problem."

Again, she didn't answer, and just turned her head to look out the passenger window. I was getting frustrated to the point of helplessness and raised my voice.

"Damn it Sue! Will you answer me?"

To my surprise, her mood changed immediately. She snapped back saying, "When I get home, come in the house with me. I'll call Delores and tell her in your presence. I'll let her be a part of it. Will that satisfy you?"

"Yes!"

Pulling into her driveway, I noticed her garage door windows were still covered from the inside. I took her remote from the glove compartment and pushed the button to open the garage door. Suddenly, she snatched it from my hand pushing the button again, sending the garage door in the opposite direction.

Surprised at her reaction, I asked. "Why did you do that?"

"I'd just rather go in through the front door. I have some things strewn on the floor of the garage," she replied.

After putting the car in park, I said, "I don't remember seeing anything strewn around. What kind of stuff is it?"

She became annoyed at my questioning her statement replying angrily, "Do you have to challenge everything I say? Do I have to tell you every little thing I do? It's becoming annoying."

"Sorry if you feel that way. You seem to have a problem with me questioning you. It's nothing more than concern on my part. If you're reading anything different, that's in your mind."

Looking at me she replied, "I know. It's just that my ex was that way."

"Well, take a good look. I'm not that man."

Getting to the front door, she retrieved her mail from the box, and we went in. As she was looking through the mail I asked, heading for the kitchen, "Would you like a cup of coffee?" she didn't answer.

I looked into the living room and could see she seemed to be engrossed in reading a letter. I asked again, "Hey, would you like a cup of coffee?"

Still reading, she gave me a wave of approval then looked up, "Yes, I'd like a cup."

Bringing them into the living room I asked, "What's the letter?"

Quickly folding it, she shoved it in her handbag.

"What's that all about? You look disturbed," I asked.

"Oh, it's nothing to be concerned about."

I knew she was lying, but with her condemnation about questioning her, I didn't pursue it any further. "How's your coffee?" I asked.

"Great. Now let me call Delores and tell her I'll be glad to have her help with my problem."

I watched as she dialed the phone, and assumed Delores picked up the receiver. I heard Sue assure Delores that anything she could contribute would be welcomed. After hanging up the phone, she looked at me and sarcastically said, "Now, does that satisfy you?"

"Frankly, yes: At least I know you'll have someone that knows more about it than me. Now, what do we do about dinner?"

"I don't really feel hungry. I think I'll pass on it," she replied.

"Is that supposed to mean you don't want my company?"

"No, it just means I'm not hungry. I think I'd rather spend the rest of the evening alone."

After finishing my coffee, I picked up my coat and I headed for the front door. Before exiting I said, "If you need me, call."

I wasn't going to give her the pleasure of seeing me upset with her rejection, and when I opened the door, I turned to look at her expecting some kind of response. I could tell it was what she wanted me to do, so I didn't disappoint her and closed the door behind me. Outside, the cold winter air felt like a tropical breeze, compared to my rejection of her company for the evening. As I was about to get in my car, I looked back at the front door. Unlike before, she didn't make an effort to even apologize. Curiosity about the garage door made me want to look, but I decided to go back to my apartment. After eating one of my frozen dinners, I decided to call Delores and thank her for wanting to help with Sue's problem. After dialing the number she answered the phone.

"Hello: Who's calling?"

"It's me. I want to thank you for wanting to help with Sue's problem."

"When did she say that?" she replied.

"Just before I left the house. She called you and said she would be grateful if you would help."

"I haven't spoken to her since you dropped us off."

"Impossible. I stood there while she dialed your number, and carried on a conversation with you."

"I assure you, Ray, she never called."

"Delores, I don't like it. She acted so cold to me when I left."

I suddenly remembered something. A small portion of one of the garage door windows became uncovered when I attempted to open it. Was I making an excuse to go back? I decided to swallow my pride and do just that.

I pulled into her driveway and looked at the garage door for a few moments, then went around my car and looked through the small opening. Peering into the darkness, I couldn't see anything out of the ordinary. Suddenly, there was a dim light. What was it? I quickly ducked down to avoid being seen.

To my surprise, Sue was standing there surveying what looked like a chalk drawn circle in the middle of the garage floor. Not being a fan of the mystique movie genre, I'd never seen a symbol of what was drawn on the floor, but knew it had something to do with the problem Sue was going through. My first reaction was to knock on the door, but instead, I decided to wait and watch. The cold air from her rejection of my company, gave way to the realization of her depth in the occult. It was greater than I, or even Delores imagined. Watching her, to my surprise, she went to a closet and retrieved a white robe. After putting it on, she stood for a few moments looking around the garage then seemed to focus on the window I was looking through. I quickly reacted by ducking down. I thought, "Did she see me psychically, or did she sense my presence?" I wasn't sure. "Should I call Delores and Don again and ask for their assistance?"

Not wanting something to occur in my absence, I went back to the front door and knocked. It took a few minutes for Sue to answer, but when she opened it, it looked as though she just awoke. It had only been 15 or 20 minutes since I left the house, and only a few minutes since I looked in the garage. Something didn't seem right.

"Ray, I thought you were going home?" she said.

I had to make a quick excuse for returning and said, "I just wanted to apologize for acting the way I did. Are you sure you're alright?"

"Yes, why don't you come in?"

I was surprised at the offer, but didn't hesitate. For a moment, I thought

I heard a few voices.

"Sue, do you have the TV or radio on in your bedroom?"

She seemed to be still in a semi-conscious state, and I had to repeat my question. Looking at me as though she just realized I was in the room, she replied, "No, I don't think so. Would you like something to drink?"

"Yes, I would," I replied, hoping I could spend more time with her.

"What would you like?" she asked.

"Anything would be fine."

I wanted the opportunity to look in her bedroom without her being suspicious and said, "Sue I have to use the bathroom."

"Go right ahead."

As I walked down the hall, I looked in each room as I passed. There didn't seem to be anything wrong, but wait! There's the blue bottle on the dresser emitting that soft glow, and there's the folder between the two candle sticks too. I realized why she didn't want my company. I was losing the battle to keep her.

After my visit to the lavatory, I returned to the living room. She came from the kitchen with an herbal tea which she sometimes drinks.

"Here, Ray, I'm fresh out of coffee, I made you an herbal tea. Will that be ok?"

I didn't question her, but remembered I made a pot of coffee when we returned home. The can still had about a third left in it. I didn't want to dispute her claim and put myself back in the dog house again, so I opted to keep quiet. I didn't know how to present it to her, that I saw her in the garage, and the chalk drawn symbol in the middle of the floor. I picked up my cup and blew on the steamy brew before taking a few sips, trying to organize my thoughts. I finally said, "Sue, I have to be honest. I saw you in the garage putting on a white robe. I also saw a large chalk circle with different symbols drawn around it, on the garage floor. What's going on?"

With a surprised look at my statement, I could tell she was at a loss for words. Looking down at the floor, she finally confessed the meetings with Justin and a few of his friends.

I asked, "What took place at the meetings?"

She looked confused at my question and replied, "I don't really remember. It all seems fuzzy to me. After I drink the brew they prepare, it's like, like, like I'm not even in my own body. I somehow rise above what's taking place. Something like when you watch a movie. You're seeing everything that's going on from the outside, but I'm physically one of the group members."

I was shocked at her confession, and suddenly realized they seem to be pulling her in by means of a drug of some sort. As I was listening, my eyes began to get heavy, and it became difficult to keep them open. I tried to get to my feet, but it seemed as though my legs couldn't support me, and fell back on the couch. I looked at my cup and realized Sue must have put something in my drink. I slapped it off the table, and tried to stand again. Without success, I fell back onto the sofa.

As my eyes became heavier I asked, "Why, Sue. Why?"

Through a foggy mist, I could see her rise from her chair. She had a blank look on her face, as though she was being involuntarily controlled by an outside force. I could hear her answer, but the words were like an echo, not really clear. I tried once again to get to my feet, but failed. Wondering why someone wanted me to be incapacitated rather than completely passed out, I couldn't guess. Could they want me to understand what they were doing, for the lack of better words?

Was I going to be the object of sacrifice? Why did Sue have to follow them?

Like looking through a hand poured piece of glass, the image of Sue appeared convoluted. She took me by the arm, and it seemed as though the power of her psychic ability, gave me the strength to stand.

Guiding me, she walked me to the bed room, and laid me on her poster bed. With leather thongs, she secured my wrists and ankles to each corner. Straining against them, I tried once again to rise but couldn't. With what was going on, I definitely thought I was going to be the sacrificial lamb. I called out her name, but she only looked. Her facial expression was as though she wanted to help, but was powerless.

I looked as she sat at the bench seat and lit the candles. Taking the folder from the drawer she opened it, and began to read the strange words. As she was reading, she began to brush out her long hair, occasionally turning to look at me.

The more she read, the brighter the blue bottle became. In my stuporous-state, I could see the images being transferred from the bottle in a strange mist, appearing in the mirror. I remembered Delores saying the bottle was some sort of connection with what I was seeing, a doorway to its past history. After Sue was finished brushing out her hair, she pulled the hood of her robe over her head.

Slowly turning, she rose from the seat and stood at the foot of the bed, continuing to read from the folder.

Focusing on her, I didn't notice at first, but the images in the mirror began to step through. First, the Civil War soldier then the Revolutionary War soldier. Terrified, I could see the blood stains still on their jackets. They took positions on either side of the bed and stared straight ahead, as if they were sentries. The next images to appear, were several robed-hooded figures. They stood in a semi-circle around the bed as Sue continued to read. I frantically kept shifting my head from side to side, thinking an attack may come at any minute. I kept yelling her name, but it seemed in vain. Whatever was controlling her was even more powerful than my plea.

Looking at the mirror again, I could see Druids in a circle, chanting and slowly moving in unison counterclockwise at what appeared to be Stonehenge. It was getting dark, but I could see plain enough to identify the scene being played out before me. Although I was in a room, the stars in the sky were like a bright canopy overhead, was it the drink that made it appear I was outside? I didn't know. The bright sky illuminated a hooded person being escorted to the center of the circle by two robed people. They left the person in the center then joined the other members. Suddenly, the chanting and movement stopped, and the person in the center pulled the hood of her robe down. To my shock, the woman looked exactly like Susan. Was this the reason she was selected? Was she that person in another life, centuries ago?

Taking the blue bottle from under her robe, she lifted it to the heavens, saying a few words I couldn't understand before she drank from it. Although there were no clouds in the sky, there was a flash of lightning seconds ahead of a roll of thunder. Was this all from the power of the blue bottle, or was it drawing power from within the stone monoliths of Stonehenge?

Beginning to chant again pulling down their hoods, I was shocked to see Justin. He seemed to be the leader of this macabre scene. Delores was right when she said. 'They can manifest themselves into what we would think were real flesh and blood beings.' When I grabbed him by the sleeve, he was real. Or was it my own mind thinking he was real. No, I was certain of it, but on the other hand, he left no identifiable marks in the snow outside the window when I pulled back the drapes.

I heard him say, "We're in danger of being discovered. We have to suspend our meetings for awhile. Suddenly there appeared to be what looked like men dressed in black, resembling pilgrims. They drew swords and held lances looking at the circle of robed people, blocking their escape. Realizing their fate, they tried to scatter, but the mounted men charged, wading into the group cutting down everyone within reach. Justin, and the person who looked like Sue, along with two others, lie on the ground pretending to be mortally wounded. One of the men dismounted. Wading through the people that were trying to crawl to safety, he stabbed them with his lance. He picked up the blue bottle and after examining it, placed it in a bag and handed it to who appeared to be the leader. He said, "Oliver, I think this is what gave them power. We did the Lord's bidding this night."

Was he referring to someone prominent back in British history? Could he be speaking to Oliver Cromwell? The way they were dressed, would fit that period, the early 1600's.

After they departed, Justin and the few survivors got up and checked the other members. Other than themselves, there didn't seem to be anyone alive, and the images slowly began to disappear. Is this why the cult turned to sacrificial gatherings, to commemorate this event? Hoping I wouldn't be the subject of this gathering, I strained against the leather thongs that held me captive, twisting and turning my wrists, but to no avail, I was held fast.

The drug I was administered was beginning to wear off, and my senses were coming back to normal. I cried out several times to Sue hoping it would snap her out of the state of limbo she was in, but my pleas for help seemed to be falling on deafened ears. Her only motion was to stare down at me with a sympathetic look. The people surrounding the bed gathered together at the foot, and I was sure they were discussing my fate.

Justin went to the bureau and picked up the blue bottle, pouring some of its contents in a glass. Handing it to the Revolutionary War soldier, he motioned to them without making comment. For the first time since they entered the room, the sentries moved, and Justin seemed to be controlling them with his psychic ability. The Civil War soldier put his hand behind my head lifting it off the pillow, and I could feel, it was cold as ice. The Revolutionary War soldier put the glass to my lips forcing me to drink. I held my lips tight together trying not to swallow the liquid entering my mouth, but he closed my nostrils with his cold fingers forcing my mouth open. I could feel the liquid in my mouth and tried hard not to swallow, but having to take a breath, I could feel the refreshingly cool liquid go down. It felt like the description Sue described, when she told us about the old woman who gave her the drink. After accomplishing their task, they returned to their former positions.

In a few minutes the room began to get misty again, and I knew the effect of the drug was taking hold. I cried out, "Sue, help me, please! These people aren't real."

She looked but didn't answer. Two of the hooded people took Sue by each arm leading her out of the room, with the other members following. Justin and the soldiers remained for what seemed like 10 minutes. I could hear a faint sound of chanting, but where was it coming from? The words were familiar. I heard them while I was listening to the ritual I witnessed at Stonehenge. Justin seemed to be listening as though he had to react at some point, and when the chanting stopped, he motioned for the soldiers to loosen my binds. Picking up the folder, he began to read the words as I was escorted with a soldier on each side, out of the room and down the hall toward the garage. I thought, "Is this where the sacrifice will take place?" More than ever, I wanted to flee and leave Susan to the fate of what these spirits wanted. Maybe it was beyond my power to help?

As we entered the garage, the robed people that were surrounding my bed, were standing around the chalk circle drawn on the floor. I was led into the center of the circle and forced to kneel. Justin handed Sue the folder, and she began to recite the same words the Druids did before being slaughtered. Looking up at her hooded face, something didn't seem right. I could see her face that was shadowed by her hood changing. Like a kaleidoscope, flashes of a foreign face, were replacing her own. Back and forth they went, and I thought it was the affect of the drug I was given. When Justin pulled back her hood, I was shocked to see the sweet kind face I caressed, being replaced by the wrinkled face of a haggard woman. If I had to guess, it was the description of the woman Sue described on the porch of the cabin that brought the soldiers back to life. When the old woman stopped reading, Justin re-entered the circle taking the folder. He spoke quietly to the old woman and I couldn't exactly hear what was being said, but I was certain they were discussing my fate.

As soon as he left the circle, the old woman opened her robe exposing a dagger. Through this whole episode, I suspected it would lead to something like this, but was hoping my pleas would affect Susan's mind, bringing her back to her senses. I tried once again in a loud voice, "Sue, please! Please help. You're not the person I'm seeing. I'm seeing the old woman that brought you into her cabin and gave you the cool drink of water." I repeated myself louder, then louder again, but it didn't seem to have any effect as she drew the dagger from the rope belt around her waist. Holding it by the blade she raised her arms skyward repeating what the Druids said just before being killed. Suddenly, the sky appeared as it had in the bedroom, and we were standing once again in Stonehenge.

The scene was exactly the same as the scene in the mirror. I knew it was the effect of the drug, but as hard as I tried, I couldn't erase the image from my mind. I thought, "If I could only concentrate hard enough, maybe it will disappear."

I struggled trying to overcome what was happening, but to no avail. She took the dagger by the handle and looked down at me. Raising it over my head, I tried once again yelling, "Sue, these people aren't real. Help me, please!"

She stopped with the dagger inches above my head, and I could see her face flashing back and forth, as if she was struggling to overcome what was happening.

Justin entered the circle once again and whispered a few words. I tried to overcome his power, by telling Sue how much she meant to me, and the life we could have together. She stopped, then looked down at me. I knew I was doing the right thing. If I could only maintain her attention until the drug they gave her wore off, I knew I might succeed.

"Sue, Please! These people aren't real, I kept repeating, these people are several hundred years old. They're spirits! They're not real," she paused again.

Justin re-entered the circle and took the knife from Sue. After giving her a stern look, she exited the circle.

Chapter 11

I looked toward the garage windows and could see the motion detector light go on. The shadows of two heads, a woman and a man were silhouetted on the sheets draped in front of the garage windows. I yelled out, "Don, is that you?"

"Yes, it's me and Delores. What's happening in there?"

"Hurry, they're going to kill me," I screamed.

I heard Don say, "Delores, you have a key, go in through the front door. Be careful, we don't know what to expect."

My cries were heard and I could see Don frantically pounding on the garage window with his fist. I could see the disturbed look on Justin's face, and it seemed more than ever he was determined to go through with this sacrifice.

I could hear Delores in the living room as she entered the house calling in a loud voice, "Sue, where are you? Are you alright? Sue! Sue! She kept repeating her plea. I could see Sue's face responding flashing back and forth from the haggard old woman, to her natural face. I knew her feelings for me and her friend were beginning to overpower Justin's compulsion to complete this ritual.

Don's forcefulness with his fist hammering on the garage window, caused the plexi-glass to give way on one corner. Continuing to yell disrupting the gathering, I could see him force his hand in, grabbing at the sheet covering the window. He was able to pull it down and must have been shocked at what he was seeing, temporarily stopping trying to absorb the scene. Justin, seeing Don making headway getting into garage, and hearing Delores in the house, was forced to abandon the ritual, and try getting to safety back through the mirror. They were filing out of the room as Don climbed through the window, and Justin directed the two soldiers to ward off any attempt Don made to hamper their retreat. After Justin left, the sentries stood on each side of the doorway, holding their rifles bayonets fixed. Their eyes blazing red, they seemed to be determined to ward off any threat to the orders they had been given. When they began to advance toward us, shocked Don hesitated in cutting the binds that were holding me.

I quickly said, "Don, these people aren't real. The only way they can accomplish what they do, is reign in someone's spirit that's alive. That's what they were doing with Susan."

As they came closer, he seemed to be mesmerized by what he was seeing. I yelled at him again to break his fear of them advancing. I could tell he wasn't sure to take my word for it, and I knew he was thinking to himself, "A mistake in my judgment could prove fatal."

Looking around, he picked up a handle of a car jack, throwing it at the civil war soldier. It struck him on the chest, but passed through hitting the wall on the other side. The soldier looked down, seemingly unaffected at it passing through his body. The Civil War soldier turned to look at the Revolutionary War soldier, then they both looked at Don, pointing their weapons at him. As they began to advance again, Don backed away frantically looking around the darkened room for another weapon. Something, anything close by, to ward off the impending doom of their wrath.

Forced into a corner, he knocked over a few cardboard boxes. They were boxes belonging to Sue's husband he hadn't had a chance to pick up. One opened, spilling the contents of WW2 paraphernalia Sue's husband's father had collected. Stumbling to get to his feet, Don's hand hit something. What was it? Hopefully something he could defend himself with. In the darkened corner, he could see it was a Japanese military sword. Taking it from the brass holder, the shiny blade seemed to temporarily halt the advance of the sentries.

Don couldn't figure out at first why, but then it dawned on him. Could this blade have a history of violence the sentries were familiar with? Could their sense of living in the spirit world give them the ability to look into the swords past deeds? Was it an implement used in the beheading of soldiers, much like themselves? Soldiers that had no choice but to do someone else's bidding?

Whatever the sword represented, in their minds, was enough to cease their advance. Don and I looked at each other as the shadows of the soldiers began to fade. After they were gone I quickly asked, "Don, where's Delores?"

He helped me to my feet, still half groggy from the potion I was forced to drink. Suddenly we heard a scream. "That sounds like Delores," Don frantically said.

I replied, "She's probably in the bedroom. That's where this ritual began. Let's go." Running down the hall we saw Justin as he was about to enter Susan's bed room. I yelled, "Justin, where's Susan? What have you done with her?"

Looking back over his shoulder, he didn't answer, but as I got closer, he was able to get the others in the room then slam the door closed. I hammered with my fist but to no avail.

Don said frantically, "I wonder if Delores is in there?"

"I don't know Don." I said, as I continued to pound on the door. I only saw Justin and one other person before him, but I'm sure they're all in there."

"I'm going to check the rest of the house just to make sure," he replied.

I stopped hammering at the door with my fist for a moment. With my ear to the door, I could hear some faint chanting as the robed Druids did when I was kneeling in the center of the sacrificial circle. I thought, "Delores must be in there taking my place." When Don came back to the hall, he verified my thought. He quickly said, "She isn't in any of the rooms, she must be inside."

I told Don my suspicions, and I could see the shock of my words in his eyes. He pounded harder calling out her name. I did likewise trying to get Sue to respond. The chanting grew louder and we could hear Delores pleading to Sue, just as I had.

"Don, we'll never get through this door. Go to the garage and see if you can get something to batter it down with, a crowbar, an axe, a sledge hammer, anything."

Leaving me to keep trying to get the door open, I kept pounding and hollering trying to disrupt the ritual. Within a few minutes, Don returned with a sledge hammer. Standing back while he took aim at the door handle, he swung the sledge with all his might. His aim was perfect, but did little damage to the thick oak door. Again, he tried without success. We kept hearing pleas from Delores to Sue, asking her to stop the madness. Realizing Sue was becoming conscious, Justin must have administered more drugs. I could only imagine Sue, being controlled by Justin, couldn't overcome her feelings for the safety of a lifelong friend. I took the sledge from Don and swung it at the hinge side of the door, until the top hinge gave way.

Through a small opening, we were able to see Delores bound hand and foot to the bed just as I had been. Susan was standing next to her with a dagger raised, poised to strike at Delores at Justin's command. The door was slowly giving way with our hammering and I yelled, "Sue, put the dagger down! Put the dagger down, for god's sake."

Justin, seeing us gaining entry, realized he couldn't continue and instructed the others to go through the mirror. As he passed through, Susan dropped the dagger and collapsed. Don loosened the binds holding Delores, and through the fear of her experience, she grabbed him. Having a delayed reaction to her near death experience, she broke down crying.

I knelt at Susan's side, and began to shake her. She slowly began to come around and said, "Where am I? what happened?"

"You've been a part of the cult ritual of the Druids. You were about to sacrifice Delores, until we broke into the room."

With a doubtful look, I could tell she wasn't aware of what was taking place. Glancing at Delores, she realized I was telling the truth.

"Where's Justin and the others?" she asked.

"Justin and the others went through the mirror. He was the last person through. That's when you dropped the dagger and fainted."

After they both recovered, the lighting in the room grew dim and finally went out. A soft glow began to fill the room emanating from the blue bottle. Brighter and brighter it grew until it appeared to be a moonlit night.

Glancing at the mirror we saw the image of what looked like young George, sitting on the floor watching his grandmother brushing out her hair, uttering the strange words George couldn't understand.

Susan said, pointing at the mirror. Look! Look! Look at the scene in the mirror George's grandmother is looking into."

I asked, "What Sue? What are you looking at?"

"The mirror she's looking into, she's seeing the ritual at Stonehenge. That's the doorway to the past. It's not the blue bottle! It's the mirror."

Unlike before, when we had difficulty seeing what Sue could see, it was a double image, like looking at a picture of someone looking at their reflection in a mirror. It was new to Delores and Don, but I watched again at the horror of the men dressed in black circling the gathering.

"What's this?" Delores asked.

I quickly commented, "Watch, this is what the ritual's all about. This was the beginning of the bottle's power."

Her and Don watched as the command was given to attack. As they waded into the crowd of worshipers, slicing down everyone within reach, Delores turned her head, not wanting to witness the spectacle. I urged her to brave looking at the scene to its entirety, so we could understand what we were dealing with. Slowly turning toward the mirror, she saw exactly what I witnessed. She saw Justin get to his feet with the remaining survivors. With raised arms, he angrily called on their god to condemn the attackers with a curse.

He said, "From the powers of our most sacred temple- I curse you and all your people. You shall have a division that will cause a civil war. The earth shall run red with your blood. Down through the centuries the curse upon this night will plague you and your families."

The few survivors gathered the bodies of their comrade's, piling them in the center of the circle. Setting them ablaze, they formed a circle offering the spirits of the dead to the heavens. The hooded shadows of the living were reflecting on the stones of their temple. The solemn offering seemed to give the dead an immortal offering of their spirit through the power of Stonehenge.

The brutality which claimed their physical lives, would live down through the centuries, Justin declared to the group.

"We must commemorate the raising of the spirits of our followers this night, with a sacrificial offering to the gods. We shall gather here each year on this date, to fulfill this sacred promise."

The flames from the deceased slowly died as dawn was breaking, and Justin instructed the others to guard against speaking to anyone about their cult under penalty of death.

Delores said, "I wonder if Susan's one of the spirits offered to the heavens, or is she one of the survivors? Was I the intended sacrifice, or was I just an innocent bystander?"

These were questions for which we had no answer. Refocusing on the image of George's grandmother, she turned motioning for Susan to enter her world. Glancing at Susan, she appeared to be falling under her spell again.

The young lad stood up in defiance of his grandmother's wishes, and as we continued to watch, he walked toward us. Coming closer with each step, he began to grow older. We realized when he was close enough to the window of the past, his reflection was real. I quickly turned to examine the room, just to clear my mind he wasn't actually with us. It was the spirit of George, the George as the old man we once knew, the kind old gentleman, with the smile on his face we remembered. Through his psychic ability, and probably his inner action with Delores and Susan, it seemed as though he transferred some of his powers to Delores. We watched as George put fourth his hand extending it from the mirror.

Without exchanging a word, Delores picked up the folder and handed it to him. He took the folder then smiled. As he walked away, he returned to the image of the small boy. He handed the folder to his grandmother, and sat on the floor beside the dressing bureau. Taking it, she placed it in front of her and began to read. As she read, the images began to return to her dressing mirror.

Not wanting to revisit the pages of history, Delores picked up the blue bottle but hesitated. The image of George in his youth suddenly looked in our direction.

Delores said sorrowfully, "I'm sorry George, there's no other way to end this; you're spirit must remain just a memory. We'll miss you, and will never forget what you opened our eyes to see." Pausing for a few more seconds as though she was cataloging to memory the scene that was before us, she hurled the bottle at the mirror. The force not only shattered the mirror, but shattered the bottle in a hundred pieces as well. Would it be able to return to its original form as it did during the last séance at the farm? Only time could tell.

With the shattering of the mirror and the bottle, Susan began to come back to normal. "What are you doing in my bedroom!" she demanded, "How did my mirror get broken?"

Looking at each other, we smiled. Delores asked, "Sue, don't you remember what's been happening for the last hour?"

"No, other than the dream I just had. It was really strange. I dreamt George came back. He stood right here. Right here with us. He was smiling at me, a smile like he gave us when you and I made him lunch Ray. Do you remember?"

"Yes, I remember. He was a great guy. I really have a lot to be thankful to him for, especially tonight."

Don added, "That's an understatement."

Susan looked at him bewildered by his remark, then asked, "Will one of you please tell me what the hell went on?"

Looking down at her feet, I suddenly realized she was bare foot. I said, "Sue, sit on the bed while I get you slippers or shoes. There's a lot of broken glass we have to clean up. Delores, why don't you go with Sue to the kitchen? Don and I will clean up this mess."

As Don began to pick up the larger pieces of the broken mirror, I went to the garage to get a trash can to put it in. I opened the inside door to the garage and a blast of cold air hit me. I had forgotten the garage door window was battered in by Don trying to gain entry, and looked around for something to cover it. Looking among the cardboard boxes, I found a box cutter and began to cut off a generous piece. As I looked at the chalked surface of the garage floor, I was reminded of the frightening experience I had. For a moment, I questioned myself. "Were the sentries real, or was it my imagination caused by the drug they gave me?"

Putting the remainder of the box down, something shinny caught my eye. "What's that?" I thought. Most of it was hidden behind another box on the stack.

I bent down and picked it up. Realizing what it was, confirmed my suspicion that in fact, the experience was real. It was a Revolutionary War bayonet. While I was examining it, Don opened the door to the garage.

"Hey, what's taking you so long?"

"The window was pushed in so I thought I'd secure it first" I replied.

"What's that you're holding?"

"It's a Revolutionary War bayonet. I found it behind this box."

"Let me see it."

Taking it, he looked it over. "That looks like the one that was flashing when they were advancing toward me. Why they suddenly stopped, I don't know. I'm just glad they did."

"Not more than me," I replied.

"Ray, do you think this was part of the military antiques Susan's husband had in that box with the Japanese sword?"

"I don't know."

Don shivered then said, "I don't know whether it's the cold air in here, or what you just said. If she doesn't recognize it, that means the whole experience was real and not a hallucination. Let's go ask."

"Ok, I'll bring the trash can. We might as well clean up that bedroom first. I think while we're at it, we should bring that bureau in the garage. I'll put it out on trash day."

"I think that's a good idea," Don replied.

Picking up the broken pieces of mirror, we found a few pieces of the blue bottle scattered among them. My first thought was to separate the pieces, so there would be no way they could reassemble. As if I was transmitting a thought, Don repeated what I was thinking.

"Maybe you're right Don. I'll put some in a bag and put them in my car. I'll dump them in the dumpster at the apartment complex."

After cleaning up the bedroom, we joined Sue and Delores in the kitchen. When we walked in, Delores asked, "Don what's that?"

"It's something Ray found on the floor in the garage. It was behind one of the boxes Sue had packed for her ex. Sue do you remember seeing this?"

Staring at it for a few moments she said, "No, I never saw that before. It's not part of the collection he had. All his antique military things are from World War 2 it was given to him by his father. He fought in the war."

"Do you mind if I keep it?" Don asked.

"No, go right ahead. In fact, if my ex doesn't pick up the rest of his things, I'll give them to you too."

Don replied, "That's ok, this is all I want. It will always be a reminder of what happened tonight."

Don and I looked at each other with a smile.

I said, "Sue, we cleaned up the bedroom as much as possible. There may still be some slivers of glass we missed, so be careful, and don't walk around without footwear. We also carried the dresser out to the garage. Don and I will come back and put it out for the trash men."

She replied, "Do you think I can get a new mirror for it? It's a really neat antique?"

"We had enough problems with the damn thing, why tempt fate?" I said.

Delores replied, "I don't think it will be a problem. The bottle no longer exists, and it was the key to the mirror. The mirror and the images it held are gone. They won't come back if the glass is different."

Looking at Don then looking skeptically at both of them, I replied, "Well we can give it a try."

Don said, "Hey! That coffee smells good. Don't we get any?"

Sue replied, "Yes, sit down, I'll pour it. After the excitement tonight I think all of us need it," she continued, "You know, Ray, I don't think I want to keep this house. Everything that's happened here makes me afraid to live in it."

Delores, giving her a surprised look, said, "Since we've gotten rid of the things that were causing the problem, I don't know why you would want to sell."

Sue replied, "It's not only what happened with me recently, it also has some bad memories of when my ex lived here. I thought about it before, and maybe the recent events are what I needed to give me that push to do it."

Realizing an opportunity I added, "Well, my apartment's available if you want it?"

Don humorously added, remembering when we checked into the motel what the desk clerk asked, "Will that be three rooms or two?"

Susan replied, "Two."

"Sue, don't worry. My apartment has two bedrooms."

We laughed and that's exactly what we needed. To my surprise, she said,

"Delores, help me get a few things together. I might as well see what my sleeping accommodations look like."

Happy at her decision, Don and I took one last look through the house. Sue came out of her bedroom carrying a small overnight bag and I asked, "Are you ready to leave?"

Raising her bag to show me she had the possessions she needed, she replied, "As ready as I'll ever be."

Taking a last look at the house as we pulled out of the driveway, Sue said, "Ray, I won't miss this house. I think part of what was happening was caused by all the bad feelings in this house over the last several years. They say evil attracts evil, and between the bureau, the blue bottle, and the bad feelings that already existed, it was like a perfect storm. My psychic ability probably had something to do with it too! I'm sure."

I replied, "I assumed you and Delores's ability had something to do with it. I think George didn't like what was about to take place, and through Delores, he gave her the idea to smash the mirror. Just before she threw it, she apologized to George, letting him know it was the only solution to saving you. He smiled at us to let her know it was fine with him."

Sue replied, "Throughout our lives, we meet people that in several days, or even hours, they're erased from our memory. Someone like George is enduring. I'll remember him for the rest of my life."

I looked down at her face and smiled, "You mean the rest of our lives don't you?"

The End

Other publications by the author:

"Veronica," a fiction murder mystery that takes place in the small resort town of Beach Haven, on Long Beach Island, New Jersey.

"Mystery of the Windowed Closet," a paranormal complete with séances, psychics and unwanted spirits.

"New Hope," a fiction murder mystery that takes place in a theatre in New Hope, Pennsylvania.

Facebook – R. J. Bonett